Dubious Deeds

Philip Ardagh gets to write this blurb himself, so whatever you read should be taken with a pinch of salt. The average person's recommended daily intake of salt is 150 tonnes. See? I warned you.

by the same author
published by Faber & Faber

FICTION

The Eddie Dickens Trilogy
Awful End
Dreadful Acts
Terrible Times

Unlikely Exploits
The Fall of Fergal
Heir of Mystery

NON-FICTION

The Hieroglyphs Handbook
Teach Yourself Ancient Egyptian

The Archaeologist's Handbook
The Insider's Guide to Digging up the Past

Did Dinosaurs Snore?
100½ Questions about Dinosaurs Answered

Why Are Castles Castle-Shaped?
100½ Questions about Castles Answered

PHILIP ARDAGH

DUBIOUS DEEDS

Book One of
The Further Adventures of Eddie Dickens

illustrated by David Roberts

faber and faber

First published in 2003
by Faber and Faber Limited
3 Queen Square, London WC1N 3AU

Typeset by Faber and Faber Limited
Printed in England by Mackays of Chatham plc, Chatham, Kent

'McMuffin' is a registered trademark of the McDonald's Corporation

A CIP record for this book
is available from the British Library

ISBN 0-571-21707-9

2 4 6 8 10 9 7 5 3 1

*This one's for
Scottish Lassie, Tessa MacGregor,
and for Aussie Sheila, Louise Sherwin-Stark.
A big professional 'thank you' to you both.*

A Message from the Author

Who's glad to be back

Eddie Dickens is back and this time he's angry! Well, that's not strictly true, but it'd be a good line to have running along the bottom of the poster if this were a movie.

Eddie's adventures didn't end with the Eddie Dickens Trilogy. Life had a lot more in store for him, and here's the first of his Further Adventures. *Dubious Deeds* finds Eddie where I am right now, in the heathery Highlands of Scotland. He may be away from the familiar surroundings of Awful End but you can be sure that his family are very much in mind.

So raise your stuffed stoats in the air and let the story commence . . .

PHILIP ARDAGH
Scotland, 2003

Contents

The Tartan Tiger

In which Eddie sets foot in a strange country and in warm horse manure

Scotland was nothing like Eddie Dickens had imagined because Eddie Dickens had never imagined Scotland. All things Scottish were all the rage when Eddie arrived in the heathery Highlands, but no one could accuse the Dickens family of being swayed by fashion. Eddie was there on business. One of Scotland's biggest fans in those days was Queen Victoria, who was on the throne at the time, except for when she nipped to the loo or made public appearances, thus giving her subjects the opportunity to try to assassinate her (which was also a popular pastime in those days). Victoria (whose first name was really Alexandrina) had a castle in Scotland and once had a Scottish ghillie as her favourite. If you're wondering whether a ghillie is fish, fowl or geological feature, I should tell you that the answer is 'none of the above'. A ghillie is a Scottish servant, and Queen Victoria's Scottish servant was a rather tall, hairy chap called John Brown who is one of the few Scottish characters in this book whose name doesn't begin with 'Mac' or 'Mc'.

The Scotsman who greeted Eddie at the tiny railway station was also very hairy but was very, very small indeed.

'I'm McFeeeeeeee,' he said, lifting Eddie's carpetbag down from the railway carriage which, if you're an American, you'd probably call a 'railroad car', but it's the same difference. Either way, it was pulled by that famous London-to-Scotland locomotive, the *Tartan Tiger*.

The way the little ginger-haired man said 'McFeeeeeeee' made Eddie suspect that it was spelled with seven 'e's, but he was wrong. There were eight and, if you don't believe me, you can count them. See?

Eddie used to travel with a large trunk but – ever since a nasty incident where Even Madder Aunt Maud (who was really his *great*-aunt) had stowed away on board a ship inside it – he now liked to travel with luggage that was smaller than his smallest relative, thus ensuring none of them could be hiding inside.

'A pleasure to meet you, Mr McFeeeeeee,' said Eddie.

'That should be eight 'e's,' said Mr McFeeeeeeee.

'I beg your pardon?' said Eddie, stepping on to the platform, closing the door of the railway carriage behind him.

'You said my name as though it were spelled with only seven 'e's, Master Edmund, and there are eight,' Angus McFeeeeeeee explained. He spoke with a very broad Scottish accent. Actually, he spoke with his mouth, but the words that came out were in broad Scots.

'I beg your pardon,' Eddie repeated, but as an apology this time rather than meaning 'what-do-you-mean?' . . . if you see what *I* mean?

3

'I forgive you,' said McFeeeeeeee, 'what with you being a wee Sassenach and all.'

'A wee whaty-what?' Eddie asked politely. He had discovered early on in life that, if you don't understand something or know what's going on, it's best to ask . . . or who knew where it might lead?

'A Sassenach is someone not from the Highlands,' explained McFeeeeeeee. 'A foreigner.'

'I've never been a foreigner before,' Eddie confessed. He didn't feel any different, which, the truth be told, made him feel a little disappointed.

'You've always been a wee foreigner to me,' the man pointed out.

'I suppose I must have been,' said Eddie. 'Funny to think that I've always been a foreigner to some people, without really thinking about it.'

Back in VR's day – VR being short for *Victoria Regina* which was Latin for 'Queen Victoria' but using up more letters of the alphabet *and* italics – the English thought that everyone else in their right minds would want to be English too, so being a foreigner was being second best. And shifty. And untrustworthy.

And here was McFeeeeeeee not only calling him a foreigner, but a wee one. Eddie knew what 'wee' meant – apart from *that*, of course. It meant 'small' and he thought it was a bit of a cheek to be called a 'wee' anything by a fully grown man who was actually smaller than he was *and* who, with that tartan tam-o'-shanter on his head, resembled nothing more than a hairy mushroom!

A tam-o'-shanter is a type of hat. (Have a look at the picture of McFeeeeeeee, which should be around here somewhere if I remembered to ask the illustrator to draw one.) Tartan – a checked pattern – requires a little more explanation but, have no fear, one of the characters will do that later, thus saving me the bother of having to do so now. (I have plants to water and cats to feed.)

Mr Angus McFeeeeeeee was the Dickens family lawyer in Scotland. Like the Queen, the Dickens family – or, to be more precise, Mad Uncle Jack and Even Madder Aunt Maud – had property in Scotland but, unlike Her Majesty, they very rarely went there. They preferred to stay in their treehouse and hollow cow, respectively, back in the garden of Awful End (where Eddie now lived with his parents).

Back in the days when Even Madder Aunt Maud was no one's mad aunt, let alone an even madder *great*-aunt, she was just plain Mad Mrs Jack Dickens. You may think that 'Jack' was an odd name for a woman, especially one called Maud, but married women were referred to by their husbands' first as well as last names. (It's true, I tell you!) If you were married to a Bill Bloggs, you were called Mrs Bill Bloggs. Before Maud had married, though, her maiden – unmarried – name had been MacMuckle so, until she and Jack Dickens tied the knot, she was plain Mad Maud MacMuckle.

('Tying the knot' is another way of saying 'getting married', by the way, and probably dates back to some strange knot-tying ritual but I've no idea what, and the thought of knot-tying doesn't excite me enough to go and look it up. If, however, string is your thing, then perhaps you could investigate this one for yourself, string and knots being so closely associated. But please leave me out of it. I don't want to get involved. Don't write and tell me the answer. *Please*. I mean it. If I really wanted to know that badly, I could always visit the Rope Museum at Mickleham Priory and see if anyone there knows. After all, rope is really very fat string, isn't it? But 'very fat string' sounds stupid, so someone came up with another name for it. And, anyway, perhaps it was a *hanky* which had a knot tied in it in this marriage ritual and not string – fat or otherwise – at all.)

Meanwhile, back in the adventure: according to Even Madder Aunt Maud, the MacMuckle family had once owned huge swathes of Scotland (not that Eddie knew what a swathe was) and a number of very fine Scottish properties. Now, however, all that was left in family hands was Tall Hall by the MacMuckle Falls, which Maud had inherited and, therefore, by law now belonged to her husband. (In other words, if a woman was lucky enough to get married back then, all she ended up with was her husband's names and all he ended up with was everything she owned: property, money, everything! Unless, of course, your name was Queen Victoria, then the rules were conveniently different.)

Apparently, Tall Hall by the MacMuckle Falls was more than just a manor house but less than a castle. The clue is in the name. The MacMuckles had started to build it with a castle in mind, and had got as far as erecting some very fine, tall walls but then the money had run out, so they put an ordinary roof on it. There were no exciting battlements or turrets. Hence Tall Hall. The MacMuckle Falls that Tall Hall was next to was rather a grand name for a rather unimpressive waterfall.

'It was more like a burst pipe than one of Nature's wonders,' Even Madder Aunt Maud had told Eddie before his departure. Soon he'd find out for himself, because Tall Hall by the MacMuckle Falls was Eddie's destination but, for impatient readers, here's a picture of both the house and the falls in the meantime:

Hasn't that nice illustrator David Roberts done a lovely job, as always? He should think about taking up drawing professionally.

Those of you who've read the Eddie Dickens Trilogy – hi there, I thought I recognised you – will be aware that, more often than not, Eddie never reaches his destination or takes a very, very long time getting there, so you may be pleasantly surprised to learn that Eddie will reach Tall Hall by the MacMuckle Falls near the beginning of Episode 3. Author's honour. Which is the same as 'scout's honour', except from an author who was never in the scouts. Perhaps I should have said 'on my honour', which is nice and old-fashioned and fits in with the feel of this 'Further Adventure'.

'When will we reach Tall Hall, Mr McFeeeeeeeee?' Eddie asked the Scottish lawyer as he followed him out of the tiny country station and into a lane, where a pony and trap was waiting for them.

'You're to spend the night in my house and tomorrow I shall take you there,' said Mr McFeeeeeeee. 'And that was nine 'e's you used just then to say my name, Master Edmund. Don't you go overdoing it now, laddie.'

'It's an unusual name, Mr McFeeeeeeee,' said Eddie, being extremely careful to get it right this time. (Angus McFeeeeeeee obviously had a very keen ear when it came to the pronunciation of his name.)

The lawyer shook his head. 'Not in these parts it ain't, laddie, though the spelling is. There's many a McFee and MacFee – with an "m-*a*-c" – in the Highlands, but ours is the only branch of the clan with quite so many 'e's.' Eddie could hear the pride in the little man's voice.

McFeeeeeeee put Eddie's carpetbag in the back of the trap and climbed into the driver's seat. Eddie jumped up behind him. With a flick of the reins, they were off.

'What exactly is a clan?' asked Eddie.

'A tribe. A family,' Angus McFeeeeeeee explained. 'My particular branch of the family were fearsome fighters. Back in the days when we were openly at war with you English, my ancestors used to be famous for jumping out of trees on to unsuspecting English soldiers riding beneath them . . . and strangling them with their bare hands.'

'H-H-How interesting,' said Eddie, politely. He looked at the tiny, mushroom-like man at the reins of the pony and trap and couldn't imagine him coming from fearsome fighter stock.

'My ancestors wanted their victims to know which clan had defeated them before they gasped their last breath,' Angus McFeeeeeeee continued. 'So, as they jumped from their treeeeeeees, they shouted McFeeeeeeee!'

'And their battle-cry became your unique branch of the family name? Amazing,' said Eddie. 'What about the MacMuckles? Did they go around killing the English too?'

The lawyer frowned, his eyebrows – like two furry ginger caterpillars – forming a 'v' above his eyes. 'There are those who claim that the MacMuckles *were* English,' he said, as though the word 'English' was something unpleasant, like dog poo. 'There're some historians who argue that they began life as the Mac-less Muckle family and that the "Mac" was added at a later date. Many a true Scot wouldnae have anything to do with them.'

Eddie thought about Even Madder Aunt Maud. She certainly didn't sound Scottish. 'Do people get on with the MacMuckles nowadays?' asked Eddie.

The trap went over a bump as the horse left the lane and set off down a rutted track. Both Angus McFeeeeeeee and Eddieeeeeeee – oops, sorry, that should, of course, be Eddie. I was wondering how long it would be before I got confused – bounced up and down on the wooden bench seat.

'Short cut,' the lawyer explained.

'The MacMuckles,' Eddie repeated. 'Do they get on with their neighbours nowadays?'

'There are no MacMuckles,' said the Scotsman. 'Well, that's not strictly true, of course. I should say that your great-aunt is the last of the MacMuckles; though, technically, she is now a Dickens.'

'The whole family – the whole clan – has died out?' asked Eddie, obviously amazed. 'I'm amazed,' he added, which he needn't have done. (I said it was *obvious* that he was, didn't I?)

'Well, they couldn't keep marrying each other and the other clans wouldnae have anything to do with them, so they eventually began to die out until only your great-aunt was left,' said the lawyer.

'Wow!' mused Eddie. 'So Even Madder Aunt

Maud is the Last of the MacMuckles of Tall Hall by the MacMuckle Falls!'

'Errrr,' said Angus McFeeeeeeee, with some embarrassment.

'What is it?' asked Eddie.

'Well . . . er . . . whilst the MacMuckles were still alive and living at Tall Hall, it was called the MacMuckle Falls but, once they'd gone, the locals renamed it.'

'So what's the waterfall called now?' Eddie asked.

'Gudger's Dump.'

'Why Gudger's Dump?' asked Eddie.

'Gudger McCloud was a poacher who made the MacMuckles' lives a misery,' confessed the lawyer, somewhat sheepishly. 'I suspect it's simply that the clans wanted to wipe out all memory of the MacMuckle name and called their so-called waterfall after Gudger to add insult in injury.'

'I get the feeling that Even Madder Aunt Maud's family weren't too popular around here,' Eddie commented.

'About as popular as a conger eel slipped down the end of a bagpipe,' agreed McFeeeeeeee.

Eddie imagined that that must be very unpopular indeed.

They reached a five-bar gate, recently painted white.

'Jump down and open that, would you, laddie?' asked the lawyer, 'whoaing' the horse.

Eddie stepped out of the trap straight on to a pile of horse manure. It was still warm.

'That's supposed to be good luck, in these parts,' Mr McFeeeeeee reassured him, but Eddie was pretty sure that he was trying not to laugh.

A Mixed Clan

*In which Eddie meets more McFeeeeeeees
and other local wildlife*

A ngus McFeeeeeeee's house seemed very small compared to Awful End and even to the house Eddie had been born in and lived in with his parents before that. (Unlike Awful End, the house Eddie was born in doesn't exist any more. This probably has something to do with the fact that it was burnt to the ground and never rebuilt. Where it once stood is now part of a business park which is probably best known for being the UK head-quarters of the company owned by the man who invented those spiky pyjamas which stop the wearer from snoring.) By local standards, however, McFeeeeeeee's house seemed large. The only other dwellings Eddie had laid eyes on during their short pony-and-trap journey were what the lawyer described as 'crofters' cottages': they were small, often round, and usually roughly thatched; the cottages, that is, not the crofters.

'What do crofters do?' Eddie had asked his travelling companion.

'Eat, sleep, drink –' began McFeeeeeeee.

'Crofting?' Eddie'd interrupted. 'What's crofting?'

'Farming,' the lawyer told him.

Mrs McFeeeeeeee was there on the doorstep to greet Master Edmund Dickens all the way from England. She was a McMuffin by birth – no relation to Dr Muffin, who'd caused that fire at the Dickens house I just mentioned, nor of the delicious breakfast products from the *McDonald's* chain of fast-food restaurants (for whom 'McMuffin', I have no doubt whatsoever, is a registered trademark). Unlike her husband, Mrs McFeeeeeeee was very welcoming indeed.

'How nice to have you here in the Highlands, Master Edmund,' she beamed. 'And how are your dear mad great-uncle and even madder great-aunt?'

'They're very well, thank you, Mrs McFeeeeeeeee –'

'Just the eight 'e's, remember,' Mr McFeeeeeeee interrupted him.

'Sorry,' said Eddie (having lost count). 'They send their regards, Mrs McFeeeeeeee.'

'How kind,' said the jolly woman, ushering Eddie into the house. 'Are they as nutty as ever?'

'As nutty as a fruitcake,' Eddie reassured her and, mark my words, fruitcakes were even nuttier in those days. You could hardly move for nuts. In fact, for a short period during Queen Victoria's reign, they might just as accurately have been called 'nutcakes' as 'fruitcakes'.

Speaking of which, the lawyer's wife now offered Eddie some refreshment. 'You must be hungry after your long journey,' she said.

'Thank you. I am a little,' Eddie confessed, 'though I did eat on the train.' His mother had made him a packed lunch comprised mainly of broad-bean sandwiches, which are, gentle readers, I promise you, as unpleasant as they sound; over-cooked broad beans, in their leathery wrinkled skins, between slices of Mrs Dickens's home-made bread.

For the Victorian poor, bread was usually the main part of their diet – in other words, mostly what they ate – and there was lots of skulduggery going on in the making of bread back then to 'bulk it out' so that the bakers could make the maximum amount of money out of the minimum amount of flour. A common trick was to add sawdust and other floor-sweepings. The well-off, however, had their own cooks and servants to make their bread for them, so could usually avoid such nasties. Eddie's mother actually liked to bake her own bread. The problem was that she also liked to add her own special ingredients, which included:

1. ground acorns
2. squirrel droppings (but only from red squirrels, not grey)
4. powdered deer's antler (stolen from one of the many mounted deer's heads on the walls of Awful End)
5. wallpaper paste (a real favourite)
6. watch springs.

Back in the days before watches were battery-powered and quartz-controlled, they had a mechanical clockwork mechanism of many moving parts, and springs were an all-important component of these works. One day, Mrs Dickens had come upon a whole drawer full of such springs and immediately put them to good use, adding a pinch of them to her bread mix every time she baked thereafter. The result? A Mrs Dickens loaf

17

of bread was probably more of a threat to your health than one sold by an unscrupulous baker; the difference being that Eddie's mother *liked* it that way. Eddie, of course, had no choice. The bread of his home-made broad-bean sandwiches was crunchy, to say the least.

Before we get back to Mrs McFeeeeeeee (formerly Miss McMuffin), I thought you might be interested to know that the sandwich was named after the person who's said to have invented the idea of putting a tasty filling between two handy-to-hold slices of bread. You would, therefore, expect that person to have been called Sandwich. It makes sense, doesn't it? If a sandwich is named after the person who invented it, then logic dictates that his name must have been Sandwich? Funnily enough, though, his name was Montagu (without an 'e' on the end). So the sandwich is named after a man called Montagu. Clear? I thought not. Perhaps I should add that he was the *Earl* of Sandwich, which is the name of a place. In fact, there's a place called Sandwich not a million miles from where I live, and there's a place called Ham near by, too. The arm of the signpost pointing in their direction used to read:

> **HAM**
> **SANDWICH** ⟩

but it was stolen so many times – by people who thought it was funny, I imagine – that it was finally replaced with one that read:

> **SANDWICH** ⟩
> **HAM**

which isn't nearly as amusing but which still makes you think.

Mrs McFeeeeeeee gave Eddie a large slice of cold game pie and some cold potatoes. 'A wee something to keep you going until supper time,' she said, handing him a large fork, before Mr McFeeeeeeee's man, McDuff, had even had time to bring in Eddie's carpetbag.

'Thank you,' said Eddie. He sat on a high-backed chair in the parlour and ate. The meal was delicious.

When Eddie had finished, Mrs McFeeeeeee asked if he'd like to have a nap, but he said that he'd like to explore. He could really do with stretching his legs after being cooped up in that train for all that time. The countryside was breathtaking, which is another way of saying that it took his breath away, which is another way of saying it made his gasp. It was so dramatic.

Although there are many different parts of Scotland with many different towns, cities and villages, it can be roughly divided into two sections: the Highlands and the Lowlands. One is much hillier and more full of mountains than the other. No prizes for guessing which is which. The Dickens house (formerly the MacMuckle house) in Scotland was, as I've already mentioned, very much in the Highlands, and so was their lawyer's home. From every window, Eddie could see moorlands covered in heather, and blue mountains cutting into the skyline on the horizon (except for from the loo window, which was made of some kind of frosted glass, which meant that Eddie couldn't see anything out of it but the failing daylight).

'Stick to the paths and you cannae go wrong,' Mrs McFeeeeeee reassured him. 'Apart from the road, the only way from here is up, so, wherever you wander, you won't lose sight of the house down below, and you'll be able to head back towards it. It also means that you'll have a nice downhill walk on your way back.'

Having once been lost on the misty moors back home, Eddie was glad that he'd be able to keep the house in sight. He set off with interest and, after about an hour, sat down on a rocky outcrop by a clump of trees and looked back down into the valley. Smoke was coming from the house's chimney.

'McFeeeeeeeeeeeeeeeeeeeeeeeeeee!' cried a high-pitched voice and someone fell out of the branches of a tree almost directly above Eddie. There was a nasty 'THUD' and a mini-version of Angus McFeeeeeeee leapt to his feet, awkwardly brushing bits of heather and dirt off his clothes.

'Were you planning to try to strangle me with your bare hands?' asked Eddie. He didn't look particularly worried for three reasons:

1. he was used to being around strange people (*a.k.a.* 'his family')
2. this boy's hands didn't look big enough to put around Eddie's neck to strangle him, bare or otherwise
3. his uncle lived in a treehouse and had fallen out of it in front of Eddie on more than one occasion, so narrowly avoiding being hit by people falling from trees could be described as a familiar occurrence in Eddie's life.

''Course not,' said the mini-McFeeeeeeee, looking a little shame-faced. He'd probably been hoping to land on Eddie, or frighten him at the very least. 'So you're the English boy, aye?'

'Yes,' said Eddie. 'Is Angus McFeeeeeeee your father? You certainly look like him.'

'Angus McFeeeeeeee is no father of mine,' snapped the boy. 'He works for *English* clients.'

'He works for my great-uncle, if that's what you mean, but I imagine that he must have plenty of Scottish clients too,' Eddie pointed out.

'If I were a lawyer, I wouldnae work for no Englishman,' said the boy. He even spoke just like a high-pitched version of Angus McFeeeeeeee.

'Were you not a wee bit surprised by my sudden appearance from above?'

'Oh, a little,' Eddie lied, politely, just to cheer up the boy. He put out his hand. 'I'm Eddie Dickens,' he said. 'Though I suspect that you already know that.'

'Magnus,' said the boy, though not shaking the offered hand.

'McFeeeeeeee?' asked Eddie. The boy nodded. 'You're not a great fan of us English then?'

'Why should we be ruled by an English queen?' squeaked Magnus defiantly.

'I think she rules most of the world,' Eddie reminded him, which wasn't far from the truth. In those days, the British Empire was spread across much of the world (except Europe) and was shown on maps and globes in pink, as though all these foreign countries were blushing with pride at being ruled over by Her Royal Highness Queen Victoria.

'It isnae right, I tell you,' Magnus muttered.

'Because she's a woman?' asked Eddie. 'Or because she's English?'

'English, of course!' said little Magnus McFeeeeeeee. 'Bertie is just as bad.' Bertie was Prince Edward, Prince of Wales, which has little to do with being a prince *in* Wales. It was simply the title given to the Queen's eldest son, who was, by birthright, first in line to throne. 'I know a riddle about him,' sniggered Magnus. 'What's the difference between the Prince of Wales, an orphan, a bald-headed man, and a gorilla?'

Eddie was shocked. He suspected that it was rather disrespectful even to try to guess the answers to riddles which included a gorilla and a member of the royal family in the same sentence. 'I've no idea,' he said. 'I think I'd better be heading back down now.' He began his descent of the sloping moorside.

Magnus McFeeeeeee ran alongside him. 'Do you give up, English?' he demanded.

'I suppose,' said Eddie, secretly intrigued by what the answer might be.

'The Prince of Wales is the heir apparent, an

orphan has ne'er a parent, a bald-headed man has no hair apparent, and the gorilla has a hairy parent.' Magnus grinned, then gave a high-pitched snort, like an excited (Scottish) piglet.

Try as hard as he might, Eddie couldn't hide his smile. Any joke with the phrase 'a hairy parent' in it was quite funny as far as he was concerned. The truth be told, it was quite a good joke for those days, and isn't too bad today, as long as you know that 'heir apparent' means 'next-in-line-to-the-throne' and that 'ne'er' means 'never'.

'Did you make that up yourself, Magnus?' Eddie asked with a sneaking admiration, trudging through the purple heather.

'I didnae,' said the mini-McFeeeeeeee, with a shake of his head. 'But here's one I did: Why will the Queen of England come in handy if you need to measure up for a pair of curtains?'

'I don't know,' said Eddie a little guiltily. 'Why will Queen Victoria come in handy if I need to measure up for a pair of curtains?'

'Because she's a ruler, stupid!' With that, Magnus McFeeeeeeee ran charging ahead of Eddie down the hill. 'McFeeeeeeeeeeeeeeeeeeee!' he yelled. If Magnus had been in charge of the original McFeeeeeeee battlecry, Eddie wondered how many 'e's that branch of the clan would have ended up with in their name.

25

By the way, I should explain that the Victorians loved a good pun. Any joke involving a play on words was seen as very clever and a bundle of laughs. By today's standards, some of them are so laboured and complicated that laughing at them is the last thing you want to do. Running away screaming, 'Enough! No more!' is the more likely reaction. Don't believe me? Then here are just three that were popular in the late 1880s (from my copy of *Old Roxbee's Appalling Puns of the 1880s*). I can only apologise in advance to anyone trying to translate these into another language – or trying to come up with equally appalling puns from the 1880s in their particular mother/father tongue – and would like to remind all concerned that I didn't make these up myself.

Q: What is the difference between a cat and a comma?
A: A cat has its claws at the end of its paws but a comma its pauses at the end of its clauses.

Groan!

Q: What fashionable game do frogs play?
A: Croaky (croquet)

Aaaargh!

*Q: Is it true that a leopard can't change his
    spots?*
*A: No, because when he becomes tired of one
    spot he can simply move to another.*

Please stop, Mr Ardagh! Please! We'll be good,
we promise! Just make the nasty jokes go away.

Okay, we'll end this episode here and begin the
next one with Eddie Dickens about to head off for
Tall Hall by the MacMuckle Falls/Gudger's
Dump. (I did promise you we would, didn't I?)

A Surprise for All Concerned

*In which the reason for Eddie's trip
to Scotland is revealed*

After a sleepless night in what he suspected was the lumpiest bed in the Highlands, if not Scotland or the entire British Empire, Eddie was up bright and early. It was the sky which was bright, I hasten to add. Not Eddie. After a night of not sleeping, his brain was particularly sluggish and, if asked what – for example – was seven plus eleven, he'd probably have replied, 'Oslo,' which is, in fact, the answer to an entirely different question altogether.

Fortunately, the only question he was asked first thing was by Mrs McFeeeeeeee (formerly Miss McMuffin) and that was: 'What would you be liking for your breakfast, m'dear?' to which he replied 'Boots and shoes' (which was actually the answer to the question: 'What is one of the main manufacturing industries in the town of Northampton?').

If Eddie's mother had been the one asking the question, then there's every possibility that Eddie would have ended up being served with boots and shoes, if she'd had the ingredients readily to hand. Fortunately for Eddie, though, Mrs McFeeeeeeee realised that he'd just spent his first night in a foreign land (if you didn't count his time at sea, which was more foreign *water*, or on a small sandy hummock mainly inhabited by turtles), so made allowances for him.

She served up some biscuits which she called bannocks and some potato cakes, all to be washed down with a big steaming mug of tea. Angus McFeeeeeeee sat at the head of the table, drinking tea from an even bigger mug, which had the effect of making him look even smaller. She sat at the other, and their son Magnus (who'd said that Angus was no father of his because he had English clients) sat opposite Eddie, giving him a glassy stare.

Living in a household where a stuffed stoat was

considered by some as an honorary member of the family, Eddie was as used to glassy stares as he was to people falling out of trees, so was equally unimpressed by Magnus's latest tactic.

'Is it true ya have a tail, English?' asked Magnus, before stuffing a forkful of potato cake into his mouth and chewing furiously.

'Magnus!' said his mother sternly.

Mr McFeeeeeeee, who was busy reading that morning's edition of the *Highlands Gazette*, either didn't hear what his son had said or pretended not to notice.

'What do you mean – ?' asked Eddie.

'Ignore the boy,' Mrs McFeeeeeeee pleaded. 'He has no manners.'

Instead, Magnus ignored her. 'I read in a book once that all you poor English have tails,' he went on. 'Like monkeys,' he smirked.

Mrs McFeeeeeeee leapt to her feet and hit Magnus with a ladle (a big spoon) which she had readily to hand. (Perhaps she often used it for this purpose.) 'Master Edmund is a guest in this house and his family are respected clients of your father,' she said. 'You're not to talk to him in this manner.'

Magnus rubbed the back of his head. 'Will ye no' keep doin' that, Ma,' he grumbled. (Aha! I was right.) 'Anyhow, English here knows I was only joking.'

'Of course you were,' said Eddie, for a quiet life. He found being called 'English' effectively annoying, but he wasn't about to admit it. He concentrated on his breakfast instead, which tasted delicious. It was often his favourite meal back home, too, because Dawkins (his father's gentleman's gentleman) was excellent at rustling up what he called 'eggy snacks'.

Mr McFeeeeeeee folded his paper in half and laid it on the breakfast table. 'Is there any more mash in the pot?' he asked. For some reason best known to himself, he called tea 'mash', so don't you go thinking there were potatoes in there too.

'You've had the last of it, Angus,' said his wife.

'Then I'll have McDuff bring round the pony and trap so as I can be takin' the boy to Tall Hall,' he said.

His wife stood up and busied herself clearing the table. Breakfast was the one meal she liked to prepare and clear away herself. Her one maid wasn't live-in and didn't usually arrive at the house until after Angus McFee had left for his office in town.

No sooner had Angus left the room than Magnus, the mini-version of himself, had snatched the paper from his place at the table. Magnus flipped through the pages until he apparently came to a story which caught his eye.

31

'Oh! It says in this here article that there's now conclusive proof that the Scots are more intelligent than the English,' he said. 'They did a series of scientific tests with a Scotsman, an Englishman, a monkey and a parrot and . . .' he pretended to read on, '. . . apparently, the Englishman came last in all of them. No surprises there, then!' Magnus grinned.

'Very funny,' sighed Eddie.

Not ten minutes later, he was in the trap with Angus McFeeeeeeee at the reins of the pony once more. When he got out to open the freshly painted white gate, Eddie was careful to be on the lookout for horse manure – steaming or otherwise – but noticed that it had already been cleared away from the night before. McFeeeeeeee rode the pony and trap through, and Eddie closed the gate, then jumped up behind the lawyer again.

The ride to Tall Hall was uneventful, but the scenery was even more dramatic than Eddie'd seen on the way to the McFeeeeeeees' house. They passed a few more crofters' cottages and saw one or two people, but for much of the time their only audience was some very shaggy-looking red-coloured cattle, with long fringes over their eyes and very large pairs of horns on their heads, and some equally shaggy-looking goats with equally impressive sets of horns. Once Eddie even thought he'd caught sight of a large-antlered deer.

Then Tall Hall came into view; the Scottish seat of the last of the MacMuckles by birth, the woman Eddie knew as Even Madder Aunt Maud. Eddie felt proud that this huge house now belonged to the Dickens family. It certainly was a strange sight with its very high walls and small windows, but with its very ordinary roof plonked down on top of it.

'Where's Gudger's Dump – I mean the MacMuckle Falls?' asked Eddie as the trap clattered up the uneven and very stony track leading to the hall. It had obviously once been a cobbled driveway, but the cobbles had been robbed out – pinched/nicked/purloined/stolen/half-inched/removed – to build other things elsewhere, and the few remaining lay like a smattering of stones found naturally in the soil.

'There,' the lawyer pointed.

It took Eddie some time to realise what McFeeeeeeee was pointing at. Today, we live in a world where Do-It-Yourself 'water features' are everywhere. Nowadays, around my neck of the woods, it's unusual to find a garden that *doesn't* have an artificial plastic-lined pond or an imitation Greek urn with water bubbling out of it, or a glass wall with a thin veil of water cascading down it, or a human-made stream flowing down steps of pebbles, all powered by an electric water pump. Back then there were really only two types of water feature: those made by Mother Nature and those made for very rich people by landscape gardeners who did things on a big scale.

Mother Nature nearly always did a good job, on a variety of scales ranging from intimate sources of springs bubbling out of the earth to dramatic, pounding waterfalls with thousands of gallons of water pouring from staggering heights. Professional gardeners created huge formal ponds, stone-statued fountains of writhing mermaids or characters from ancient Greek mythology, with jets of water spraying here, there and everywhere.

The name Gudger's Dump certainly suited what Eddie saw before him far better than the grandly entitled MacMuckle Falls. It looked like a dribbling bog; an accident . . . a puddle left by a passing herd of elephants. It was also slimy, black and horrible.

Reaching the front of the house, Angus McFeeeeeeee pulled the horse to a halt, jumped down from his seat, adjusted his tam-o'-shanter to a more jaunty angle on his head, and produced a large key from his pocket. He handed it to Eddie, who had jumped down beside him on the gravel.

'Would ya like to do the honours?' he asked.

Eddie took the key. 'Thank you,' he said.

They strode together across the driveway.

Eddie's Scottish mission was a clear one. He was to visit Tall Hall and take a look around to see what state everything was in. He was to check that the furniture wasn't rotten and the roof fallen in, for example, and to see which – if any – items were worth boxing and sending down to Awful End. They were planning to sell the last of the MacMuckle property.

'A house in Scotland's no use to me,' Even Madder Aunt Maud had told Eddie before his departure. 'I have all I need here. My Malcolm. My Jack. My shiny things and, of course, my Marjorie.' She patted a wall. 'What more could a woman need?' She picked up a large glass eye from a bowl of assorted shiny things and popped it in her mouth, sucking it like a gobstopper.

35

The Malcolm she was referring to was her stuffed stoat who went with her just about everywhere. 'Her Jack' was her husband, Mad Uncle Jack. Her shiny things were . . . shiny things. She liked shiny things. She begged, borrowed and even (sometimes) stole them. And Marjorie? She was the large hollow wooden cow she lived in and that she and Eddie were sitting inside at the time. Her walls were papered with what looked to Eddie suspiciously like shredded American one-thousand-dollar bills, but that couldn't be right. Could it?

Eddie's great-uncle had been equally dismissive about Tall Hall. 'I have no need of a home all the way up there,' he said. 'It might be different if it had a lake full of fish, of course. One can never have too much fish . . . but, as far as I can recall from my single visit, many years before you were born, Melony –'

'Eddie,' Eddie corrected him. Melony was the name of a girl who came every other month to oil the hinge on Mr Dickens's pocket knife.

'– and there was no lake and no fish. No fish I say!'

It wasn't that Mad Uncle Jack enjoyed fishing –

36

I'm not sure whether he went fishing in his entire life – it's just that (with the exception of the dried swordfish he now carried about with him in his jacket pocket, as a back-scratcher and ear cleaner) he used dried fish as a method of payment. Please don't ask. I have no idea why.

Eddie's father, Mr Dickens, had also seemed to think that getting rid of Tall Hall was a good idea. 'Any nice pieces of furniture can be brought back to Awful End and the rest sold with the house,' he said. 'Some of the money made from the sale can go towards my buying new materials.'

These 'new materials' were for his latest hobby: sculpting. Having painted the ceiling of the hall at Awful End, he had recently turned his attention to this different art form. The general consensus is that his painting abilities were worse than awful. Unfortunately, his sculpting abilities were worse still. (Mad Uncle Jack did a little and was a whole lot better.)

Mr Dickens had started on a small scale, carving the corks from wine bottles into Great Characters From History. In his eagerness to carve, he'd opened a great many bottles of wine from the Awful End cellars and, not wanting to waste their contents, often drank them before letting carving commence.

Mr Dickens's cork-carvings were bad enough when he was sober. Imagine what they were like after he'd had too much to drink. A few of them survive today (in the archives of the Society of Amateur Sculptors, Bricklayers and Dramatists, in Manchester), and I for one find it extremely difficult to tell which way up they should be. Julius Caesar's feet, for instance, look remarkably similar to his head.

Another problem with Mr Dickens carving whilst under the influence of alcohol was that he was forever cutting himself. He now had bandages on most fingers. But that hadn't stopped him starting work on a whole new scale. He'd gone from carving corks to carving logs and had even had one of the ex-soldiers who often helped out at Awful End chop down an oak tree in the grounds. Although the falling tree had destroyed the orangery – a very fancy greenhouse – the old gardener's cottage (though, fortunately, there was no old gardener in it at the time) and part of the stable block, no one seemed to mind and Mr Dickens had plenty of wood to work with.

His greatest triumph up to that time was carved from the main trunk of the tree. It was, according to him, a statue of his son, Eddie, on the back of a turtle. Although it was finally used as firewood in the great winter of '98, there is in existence a photograph of it taken by the world-famous photographer Wolfe Tablet. The picture is dark and grainy but you can still clearly see that the sculpture looks like a badly carved liver sausage on the back of a huge – equally badly carved – bowler hat.

As for Eddie's mother's opinion about what should be done with Tall Hall, she didn't have one. When Eddie'd asked her about it, she'd been far too busy trying to wash the dirt out of a piece of coal.

'I just can't get this black off,' she'd said, scrubbing it with a nailbrush.

So there it was: all four members of Eddie's immediate family happy to sell off Tall Hall. Having heard from Angus McFeeeeeeee what the locals had thought of the MacMuckles, and having seen what young Magnus's attitude was towards the English in general, Eddie didn't think there'd be any tears shed if the house were put up for sale . . . as long as, of course, a Scot bought it.

Eddie mounted the two stone steps to the front door and put the key in the lock.

'McFeeeeeee!' cried a voice, and Eddie turned in time to see a huge horse thundering across the open ground straight towards them, steam rising from its flared nostrils. It appeared to be being ridden by . . . by a headless horseman!

A Clash of Wills

*In which Eddie waves a temporary bye-bye to his
lawyer and meets some strange fruit-eaters*

Angus McFeeeeeeee's reaction to the headless
apparition was rather different to Eddie's.
Whereas Eddie recoiled in horror, not quite
believing his eyes, the lawyer simply strode
purposefully across the grass towards the oncoming
horse.

'What is it, man?' he demanded in his broad
Scottish accent.

'McFeeeeeeee!' the voice repeated, and it
suddenly occurred to Eddie that headless horsemen

wouldn't have mouths (on account of having no heads) so were unlikely to be able to shout 'McFeeeeeeee', especially with exactly the right number of 'e's. This last point led Eddie to further deduce that it was likely that McFeeeeeeee was known to the horseman and that, by McFeeeeeeee's behaviour, the horseman, in turn, was known to McFeeeeeeee.

The rider dismounted and landed on the springy turf with quite a thud. Now that he was at Eddie's eye level, all became clear. The newcomer was a small man but with a very high collar and large neckerchief (which is a cross between a scarf and a tie, and unlike a handkerchief – which is for the hand or, maybe, the nose – was for the *neck*). Having such a short neck, the man's head was almost completely obscured by his monstrous collar!

'What's the matter, McCrumb?' McFeeeeeeee asked.

'It's Mary MacHine,' said McCrumb. 'A piano's fallen on her. It doesnae look like she'll survive.'

'I'm a lawyer, not a priest,' said McFeeeeeeee, which Eddie thought was rather unsympathetic. If he were ever squashed by a piano, he hoped that the news would, at least, merit an 'I'm sorry to hear that.'

'It's not spiritual help she's after, man: she wants you to change the will!' said McCrumb. 'You must hurry.'

The lawyer still seemed a little reluctant to leave Eddie. 'She only wrote her new will at the end of last month. Why would she want to change it now?'

'She wants to write Mungo McDougal out of it. She doesnae want the man to get a single brass farthing!'

(A farthing, brass or otherwise, was the coin with the lowest value of all coins or notes/bills in Britain; it was a quarter of one penny, or half a halfpenny, which was called a ha'penny. And don't you go thinking that there were a hundred pennies to the pound. Oh, no. That would be faaaaaaaaar too simple. There were twelve pennies to a shilling and twenty shillings to the pound, which means – if this calculator's still working properly – that there were 240 pennies to the pound back then. And not only back then, come to think of it. There were 240 pennies to the pound when I was growing up, and I'm not that old. There aren't *that* many white hairs in this beard of mine, yet.)

A look of surprise crossed McFeeeeeeee's face, and got lost somewhere in those bushy eyebrows of his. 'But Mungo McDougal's forever buying Mary MacHine presents. I thought she liked the man.'

'It was he who bought her the piano . . .' McCrumb explained. 'It was riddled with woodworm.'

'Hence its collapse?' asked McFeeeeeeee.

'Hence its collapse,' McCrumb confirmed.

'Oh,' said Angus McFeeeeeeee.

Eddie came to a quick decision. 'If you must go to Mrs MacHine, Mr McFeeeeeeee, then go you must. I'll be fine here, going through the house on my own.'

'I'll ride with Mr McCrumb on his horse and leave you the pony and trap –' suggested the lawyer.

'No, don't worry, sir,' said Eddie. 'You can come back for me later when your work is done.' The truth be told, Eddie preferred the idea of going through Tall Hall his own. That way he could spend as much or as little time in a room as he wanted. He could explore exactly how *he* wanted to explore.

'If you're sure,' said Angus McFeeeeeee doubtfully.

'The boy's sure!' said McCrumb, placing his foot in his stirrup and swinging himself back on to his mount. Up on his horse, his head looked invisible to Eddie once again. 'Now hurry, McFeeeeeee. It's a *grand* piano and Mrs MacHine may soon breathe her last!'

Angus McFeeeeeee, one hand on his tam-o'-shanter to keep it in place, ran back down the driveway and into the pony and trap. With a flick of the reins he was rattling after McCrumb across the grass.

Eddie climbed back up the two stone steps, which looked like they were sagging in the middle where they'd been worn by hundreds of years of treading feet, and turned the key in the lock. The huge oak door swung open with a creak that would have delighted the sound-effects department of a film crew making a horror movie.

★

Whatever Eddie expected to find inside, it wasn't a room with people in it. The front door opened straight into a great hall with a high hammer-beamed ceiling and a huge table in the centre which was probably long enough to seat about sixty people. As it was, there were six people

45

seated around it at one end, and that was enough of a shock.

'Who are you?' asked a very puzzled and surprised Eddie.

A woman seated near the head of the table got to her feet and glided across the stone-flagged floor towards him. 'I think you'll find the question should be who are *you*, laddie?' She prodded Eddie with the tip of the long fingernail of her index finger.

'Me . . . I'm – er –' Eddie had been wrong-footed but quickly regained his composure. 'No, I think the question's still who are *you*?' He looked back at the others, still seated around the table.

They appeared to be eating a meal consisting entirely of fruit and nuts.

Eddie put his hand in his pocket and pulled out a fob watch on a chain. This was in the days before wristwatches, remember; though, by a quirk of fate, when he'd been aboard a ship named the *Pompous Pig*, Eddie had met the man who would later invent the steam wristwatch. (For those storing information for future use, the inventor's name was Tobias Belch.) On the back of this particular fob watch were the words:

To Maud
Happy 2nd Birthday
Jack

because it had been lent to Eddie by his great-aunt, Mad Uncle Jack having given it to her for her twenty-first birthday (ignore the '2nd' part!). Back in the days when she was still known as plain Mad Aunt Maud – before she'd become even madder – this self-same watch had indirectly led to Eddie being locked up in St Horrid's Home for Grateful Orphans.

Life can be strange like that. It's to do with something called either 'cause and effect' or 'the Chaos Theory'. Both work on the principle that someone picking his or her nose in South Africa can have an effect on politics in China, if the wind's blowing in the right direction . . . or something like that. I wasn't giving the subject my undivided attention when it was being discussed on the radio the other day.

Eddie checked the time. It was just gone eleven o'clock, so he couldn't tell whether these people, whoever they were, were having a late breakfast, an early lunch or something in between. They came in all shapes and sizes but, apart from the fruit-eating, all had one thing in common. They were all wearing tartan – checked – clothing. But none of it matched.

For example, the woman who'd come over and prodded Eddie was wearing a black dress with a tartan shawl that was predominantly (mainly) green and black squares. The two women at the table (whom Eddie was later to discover were mother and daughter) were both wearing mainly red tartans, but the mother – who was almost as wide as she was tall – was wearing a much stripier tartan than her daughter's (which was more 'boxy'). As you can gather, tartans aren't the easiest things to describe. The three men at the table, all of whom had enormous beards, were wearing predominantly orange, blue and black tartans. The overall effect was of a television with the colour-balance turned up too high and everyone looking over-bright and zingy (although, with television not having been invented yet, this would have been a meaningless comparison to Eddie).

The tall woman in the black dress still hadn't answered Eddie's question, so Eddie tried a different approach. 'My name is Edmund Dickens,' he said. 'I am the great-nephew of the very last of the MacMuckles, the owners of Tall Hall and I was – er – wondering what you're all doing here.'

The bearded man at the head of the table stood up, the legs of his enormous carved chair scraping across the stone flagging, causing a sound with an effect not dissimilar to someone scratching their fingernails down a blackboard, and setting Eddie's teeth on edge. The man strode over to the woman's side and glared down at Eddie. He looked like an angry mountain, if there are such things. Volcanoes, perhaps?

'The last of the MacMuckles?' he said, sounding very indignant indeed. 'The *last* of the MacMuckles? I think not.'

There were murmurs of agreement from those still at the table, like when Members of Parliament say, 'Hear! Hear!' when they agree with whoever's speaking at the time.

'Young man,' said the mountain of a man, leaning so far forward that the wispy end of his thick black beard tickled Eddie's forehead, 'we, the assembled company, are the last of the MacMuckles.'

Many a MacMuckle . . .

*In which Eddie is given a local history lesson
and a punch on the nose*

To say that Eddie 'was surprised' by the man's statement would be like saying that if someone tied your hands and feet together, filled each and every one of your pockets with rocks, chained you to a block of concrete and then threw you in a flooded mine shaft that you'd 'get a little wet'.

In modern parlance, Eddie was jaw-droppingly gob-smacked. He was stunned. His mind was boggled. He could hardly believe what he was hearing but, his mother having cleaned out both of his ears with a broad bean soaked in alcohol (attached to the end of a crochet needle), just two nights previously, he accepted that his ears were operating at 100 per cent efficiency.

'You're a MacMuckle?' he gasped.

'We all are!' said the other five, in chorus. All of them spoke with broad Scottish accents.

'This is Alexander MacMuckle, Clan Chief of the MacMuckles,' said the woman, nodding in the direction of the fierce-looking bearded man towering above Eddie.

'What's all this nonsense about your great-aunt being the last MacMuckle?' he demanded.

'I – er – Before she was married she was called Mad Maud MacMuckle,' Eddie explained.

A look passed between the woman and Alexander MacMuckle.

'Mad Maud MacMuckle?' asked Alexander Muckle.

'Well, I suppose she's Mrs Jack Dickens now,' said Eddie. 'But we all call her Even Madder Aunt Maud . . . except for Mad Uncle Jack – Mad Mr Jack Dickens – that is. He calls her love pumpkin and my little couchy-coo and suchlike.' As he spoke, Eddie realised that if *anyone* was going to get confused about being last in the line of MacMuckles when there were actually other MacMuckles still out there, it'd be Even Madder Aunt Maud. Even Mad

Uncle Jack had been rather vague about the whole thing. When, back at Awful End and up in his treehouse, Eddie had asked him about the MacMuckles, MUJ had started drawing a family tree but, when it began to look a bit like a scarecrow with straw hair and twigs-for-fingers, that's what he turned it into a picture of . . . and then coloured it in . . . and *then* put it up in his study next to a drawing of a frog which had once started out as a map showing Eddie how to get to somewhere (though he could no longer remember where).

'I – I see,' said the woman, who clearly didn't.

'Who was Maud MacMuckle's father?' asked Alexander MacMuckle, looking less stern and more confused.

'That would be Mad Fraser MacMuckle,' said Eddie. 'I think he'd have been my great-great-uncle, but he died a long, long time ago.'

'Well,' said Magnus MacMuckle, 'any relative of a MacMuckle is welcome in Tall Hall –'

'– by the MacMuckle Falls,' chanted the others.

Eddie wondered if these MacMuckles knew that it'd been renamed 'Gudger's Dump', and what they'd have to say about it.

'This is my sister Martha MacMuckle,' Alexander MacMuckle said, putting his arm around the tall woman in the black dress. 'Won't you come and sit with us, Master Dickens?'

His head still reeling at what all this might mean, Eddie followed them over to the table where an extra place was hastily laid for him.

The very wide woman introduced herself as Nelly MacMuckle and the blushing girl next to her as her daughter Roberta. She proffered Eddie a bowl of fruit. He chose an apple.

'Thank you,' he said.

'We're vegetarians you see, dear,' she said.

'But this is a fruit, not a vegetable,' Eddie responded. Vegetarians were much rarer in Britain then than they are now.

'What Nelly means is that we don't eat meat,' explained another of the bearded men, who said that his name was 'Iain with two 'i's, unlike that Englishman Lord Nelson who only had one.' I warned you that puns were popular back then. (It helps if you know that Lord Nelson was a one-eyed

54

admiral.) Although Iain probably made the same joke every time he said his name, he laughed heartily.

Soon all six of them had introduced themselves as: Alexander, Martha, Nelly, Iain, Hamish and Roberta MacMuckle.

'I thought everyone in the same clan wore the same tartan,' said Eddie, between bites of his apple. It was delicious.

Martha MacMuckle snorted. 'And that all the men wore kilts, I suppose?'

'Let me tell you a wee bit about clan tartans,' boomed Alexander MacMuckle, cutting into a pear with a small bone-handled knife. 'Have ye heard of a fella by the name of Sir Walter Scott?'

Eddie shook his head. 'But with a name like that he certainly sounds Scottish,' he said.

'Well, not that long ago' (if you must know, dear readers, the year was 1822), 'Sir Walter was put in charge of organising an event where the Clan Chiefs – the heads of the various families – would be presented to King George IV . . .' At the mention of the previous monarch's name, there was much mumbling under the assembled company's breath. Eddie got the distinct impression that the British royal family weren't the most popular people in Tall Hall. 'The event was intended to be dramatic and romantic and full of pageantry –'

'You English like pageantry,' said Nelly with a stern look on her face which would have said (if looks could speak), 'And we all know that pageantry is not a good thing.'

'So Sir Walter laid down a few ground rules. He decided that each clan should have its own special tartan and the particular patterns were decided then and there,' said Alexander.

'Many of them were made up on the spot!' said Martha.

'But I thought they were traditional designs going back hundreds of years!' said Eddie.

'So do most people,' said Nelly. 'There's been *breacan* – tartan – around Scotland for centuries, but nothing as organised and regimented until recent times, laddie, with particular setts for particular clans.'

'Setts?' asked Eddie, surprising himself by remembering that this was the proper name for badgers' burrows.

'Patterns,' growled Alexander MacMuckle.

'And many of them have only recently been made up?' Eddie gasped.

The MacMuckles nodded as one. And how right they were. The belief that this fairly modern idea is steeped in ancient Celtic history is how, in the twenty-first century, there comes to be a whole Scottish industry grown up around people who believe they have Scottish ancestry buying rugs, shawls, tam-o'-shanters, kilts and so on in particular tartans closest to their names. 'Smith?' the helpful Scottish shop assistant, grins. 'Oh, that's a well-known corruption of the Scottish name MacSplurge, and entitles you to wear the clan tartan. We have a very fine range of items in the tartan, including this superb machine-made imitation-leather keyring for just one hundred and thirty-five dollars,' which is a fine thing for the Scottish economy.

'What about kilts?' asked Eddie, thinking about the pleated tartan skirt he'd seen his great-great-uncle Mad Fraser MacMuckle wearing in the oil painting Even Madder Aunt Maud had hanging upside-down at the head of her bed inside Marjorie.

'A genuinely ancient form of Scottish dress?' asked Martha MacMuckle with a look of contempt.

'Invented by an Englishman named Thomas Rawlinson in 1768,' said her brother. 'We Scots only started making a point of wearing them when you English banned them, thus makin' it a matter of honour!'

There was a cheer from the others around the table, resulting in some of those who were still eating showering the others with half-chewed bits of fruit and nut. The spitees (if there is such a word) swore at the spitters in colourful Scots.

Eddie wondered what Mr McFeeeeeeee would make of these MacMuckles. There he was thinking that his client, Even Madder Aunt Maud, was the last of the MacMuckles and that she and Mad Uncle Jack were the rightful owners of Tall Hall . . . yet here was a whole different branch of the MacMuckle family, including one who claimed to be the Clan Chief. Not only that, McFeeeeeeee had suggested that the MacMuckles had been either English or supporters of the English, but *these* particular MacMuckles seemed as pro-Scottish and anti-Queen Victoria as Angus McFeeeeeeee's own son Magnus!

The history lesson over, Eddie thought it best to mention what was worrying him about suddenly discovering that he had a whole bunch of distant relatives whom, less than an hour before, he hadn't even known existed. 'Er, Mr MacMuckle –' he began.

'Yes?' replied Alexander, Iain and Hamish, three pairs of eyes on him at once.

'I meant *you*, sir,' he said, addressing himself to Alexander, him having been introduced as the Clan Chief and being therefore, Eddie supposed, the most important person in the room.

'Yes, laddie, what is it? What's prayin' on your mind?'

Eddie knew that this next part would be awkward but, having once ended up being arrested and (wrongly) put in an orphanage, rather than break a promise and, therefore, bring possible shame to the Dickens family, he knew that he must stake the Dickens claim. 'I'm afraid you can't – er – stay here . . . any of you. I came to Tall Hall in advance of my great-aunt and great-uncle putting it up for sale.'

There was a loud clatter as Hamish MacMuckle, by far the smallest of the MacMuckles but with the biggest, reddest beard Eddie had ever seen (and would ever see), dropped the pewter platter he was holding to the stone floor. Walnuts shattered and skidded across the huge flagstones.

Alexander MacMuckle was back on his feet at the head of the table. He glared at Eddie so effectively that it makes one wonder whether he'd been practising in the mirror or taking special night classes. 'Tall Hall is not for Mad Fraser MacMuckle's daughter to sell!' he shouted – yes, shouted. 'This place is MINE, I tell you. It belongs to ME.'

Eddie knew that it would be very silly of him to argue.

Martha MacMuckle put a calming hand on Alexander's shoulder and he sank back into his seat – rather like a throne – shaking with anger.

'Forgive my brother,' she said, 'but surely you can understand his upset?'

Little Hamish stomped over to Eddie and, to everyone's amazement, punched him on the nose. More surprised than hurt, Eddie staggered backwards and landed on his bottom with a jarring bump. Hamish stomped back to his place.

Moments later, Roberta MacMuckle was helping up Eddie. She handed him a lacy hanky she'd had tucked up the left sleeve of her blouse. 'Your nose is bleeding, Master Eddie,' she said.

He took the hanky and pressed it to his nose. It smelt of heather. 'Thank you, Miss Roberta,' he said.

'My friends call me Robbie,' she said.

'Thank you, Robbie,' said Eddie.

Roberta smiled. Eddie smiled. He thought she was rather pretty.

Just then, Angus McFeeeeeeee came charging through the front door. He stopped dead in his tracks (which may be a cliché but describes exactly what happened). 'What the devil's going on here?' he demanded.

Disputed Deeds

*In which Eddie gets a guided tour and a
right royal surprise*

'You didnae waste your time in throwin' a party,
Master Edmund!' said Angus McFeeeeeeee
in obvious amazement. 'Are you not going to
introduce me to your friends?'

'These are no friends of mine, Mr
McFeeeeeeee,' began Eddie, then, realising that
this sounded rather ruder than he'd intended,
quickly added: 'What I meant to say was that they
were here when I arrived.'

The lawyer raised one of his caterpillar-like

eyebrows into a quizzical arch. 'Were they indeed? We appear to have a clear-cut case of breaking and entering. Well,' he said, now confronting the assembled MacMuckles. 'What do you have to say for yourselves?'

'What I have to say,' said Alexander, 'is that a wee chap like you should be extremely careful who you go accusin' of breakin' and entering!'

Something changed in Angus McFeeeeeeee and Eddie could suddenly picture him falling from a tree with the cry of 'McFeeeeeeee!' on his lips and his bare hands around the neck of his enemy. 'I may appear small to you, sir!' he breathed heavily, 'but I have the might of the Law on my side!'

Nelly MacMuckle stepped between the two feuding men, filling the space quite nicely.

'Gentlemen, gentlemen!' she said. 'There's no need for this. Alexander, you must simply explain the situation to Mr –'

'This is Mr Angus McFeeeeeeee, my family's lawyer,' said Eddie.

'– to Mr McFeeeeeeee. He can't know the facts until you give them to him now, can he? Fruit?' Nelly thrust the bowl right under McFeeeeeeee's nose.

He seemed disarmed. 'What? Er – no, thank you.' It was hard to be angry when fruit was on offer. A nice apple can sometimes have a calming effect on even the most angry of people.

'You see, Mr McFeeeeee –' began Eddie.

'McFeeeeeeee,' McFeeeeeeee corrected him.

'This is Mr Alexander MacMuckle, Clan Chief of the MacMuckles. He claims that Tall Hall isn't Mad Uncle Jack's and Even Madder Aunt Maud's to sell. He says it belongs to him.'

The lawyer's eyes narrowed. 'And I suppose you have papers to prove it, sir? And I am using the term *sir* loosely!'

'To prove what exactly, Mr McFeeeeeeee?'

'That you're a MacMuckle. That you're the Clan Chief and that you have a right to this property. I hold the deeds to this house and lands on behalf of Mad Mrs Jack Dickens, formerly Mad Maud MacMuckle . . . and possession is nine-tenths of the law. Where's your documentation, Mr MacMuckle?'

'I usually find that in any dispute *this* puts across my point of view most effectively,' said the now red-faced Alexander MacMuckle, waving his huge fist in the lawyer's face.

Little Hamish wandered over and was about to bop McFeeeeeeee on the nose, in the same way that he had Eddie, when Martha MacMuckle grabbed his wrist with her long, slender fingers (including the one with which she had so successfully prodded Eddie on his arrival).

'Stop acting like children, the lot of you!' she pleaded. 'We cannae go on like this!'

This had the desired effect and, over the next half an hour or so, Eddie and McFeeeeeeee sat with the six MacMuckles or, if the lawyer's suspicions were correct, the six people *claiming* to be MacMuckles, and each side heard the other's explanation as to the state of affairs: Eddie and McFeeeeeeee were under the impression that Even Madder Aunt Maud was the last of the MacMuckles and, as her husband, Mad Uncle Jack was therefore the rightful owner of the hall, its contents and lands, and could do with them as he pleased; Alexander claimed that he and the others were all MacMuckles and, as Clan Chief, the hall was rightfully his and couldn't therefore be sold.

Eddie was simply relieved that there was no more nose-punching or fist-waving. Nutty though his family undoubtedly was, the most aggressive any of them ever got was when Even Madder Aunt Maud hit or prodded people with her stuffed stoat Malcolm.

Though once a leader-of-men in the army (and some of them were still hanging around following him all these years later), Mad Uncle Jack had claimed never to have fired a shot in anger, which was probably true because my research has uncovered the fact that he could never load his rifle properly and that the man who was supposed to do it for him – a Welshman named Private Evan Topping – used to fill it with wads of blotting paper (which he kept hidden in his kitbag for this specific purpose) because, his commanding officer or not, he didn't trust Mad Major Dickens with a loaded weapon. It is, I suspect, thanks to Private Topping that more people didn't die in Mad Uncle Jack's regiment.

True, Eddie's father, Mr Dickens, had once blown up his bedroom, but that had been as a result of lighting an early-morning cigar when the gas from a lamp had been left on.

True, Eddie's mother, Mrs Dickens, had killed Private Gorey (retired) in the sunken garden at Awful End when she'd thrown a mortar shell

66

over a wall, but that had been an accident.

As for being on the receiving end of violence, Even Madder Aunt Maud had once been hit by a hot-air balloon (which she rather enjoyed) and chased by peelers (policemen) with dogs through a hawthorn hedge. (As you can see, there's a picture of this below. It first appeared in another one of my books, in which I described the incident, but I liked it so much I wanted to give those of you who've never seen it before a chance to have a look at it, and those of you who *have*, a chance to enjoy it for a second time. I'm kind-hearted like that.)

Back to the receiving end of violence. Mad Uncle Jack had been stabbed in the bottom with a toasting fork and regularly fell out of his treehouse, and both of Eddie's parents had been victims of the two explosions already outlined, and Eddie himself had been kidnapped by escaped convicts once and locked up in that orphanage and a police cell or two . . .

. . . but, otherwise, he and his family had never really been touched by violence. Eddie suspected that this was not the case with the MacMuckles, who seemed almost eager to get involved in fisticuffs, as his nose attested. Well, the male MacMuckles, anyway. He looked across the table at Miss Roberta – Robbie – and caught her looking at him. She looked down at her lap, blushing.

Angus McFeeeeeeee was very keen that the MacMuckles 'or whoever they are' leave Tall Hall whilst the matter was being resolved. As far as he was concerned, it was down to them to prove their right to the property and not the other way around, the house having been in the Dickenses' hands for many years without anyone contesting their right, and with the deeds in his safe at his office in town.

'If we let them stay, they may refuse to leave. They may steal property rightfully belonging to your family. They may –'

'And how do you intend to get them out?' Eddie interrupted the lawyer. They were whispering in a dusty corner of the great hall, below one of the many stags' heads mounted on the wall; one of the hundreds of victims of MacMuckle hunts over the years. 'Will you bring in the police? We could end up with a full-scale battle on our hands, Mr McFeeeeeeee! I know that you're a lawyer and I'm just a boy but I'm here representing my family, and . . . and I think it'd be best if we let the MacMuckles stay here while everything gets sorted out. The house'd be empty otherwise, anyway.'

'Very well,' said Angus McFeeeeeeee, somewhat reluctantly, 'but I'll have to write to your great-uncle for further instructions.'

With the news that the Dickenses' lawyer wasn't about to try to have them thrown out, the MacMuckles became civil once more; almost friendly, some of them.

'I'd like to stay and look around Tall Hall, whoever it rightfully belongs to,' said Eddie.

'Can I show him?' asked Robbie.

Nelly, the girl's mother, shook her head. 'No, let Hamish,' she said, 'by way of an apology for what he did to ya, laddie.'

Eddie would far rather have had the guided tour from the heather-smelling Miss Roberta than the hairy nose-puncher. (By putting a hyphen between the words 'nose' and 'puncher', I'm making it clear that it's the nose-puncher who was hairy and not the noses he punched. If he were a non-hairy puncher of hairy noses, I would have written either 'hairy nose puncher' without any hyphens or 'hairy-nose puncher' like this. If he were a hairy puncher of hairy noses, I would probably have given up altogether. As for describing Robbie/Roberta as 'heather-smelling', there's a problem in English that 'smelling' can mean to smell something (as in 'he smells the cheese') or to smell of something (as in 'he smells *of* cheese') which is why this old joke works:

MAUD: My Malcolm has no nose.
EDDIE: How does he smell?
MAUD: Stoaty.

In this instance, I mean that Robbie smelt of heather (as did her hanky) because she was wearing toilet water, which may sound like something that needs mopping up but was, in this case, water with crushed heather in it, making a kind of weak smelling-of-heather perfume. She may, of course, have gone out of her way to run through the wild heather, rubbing her hands against the flowers to release their scent and sniff it in, but that's not what I meant.

Phew! I'm pleased to have clarified that.

★

It didn't take Eddie long to realise who little Hamish MacMuckle reminded him of. Why, it was young Magnus McFeeeeeeee, of course: the lawyer's son. Admittedly, Magnus didn't have a great big red beard covering most of his face and hadn't (yet) punched Eddie on the nose, but Eddie suspected that he'd very much like to, what with Eddie being English and all that! Both Hamish and Magnus reminded Eddie of coiled springs – not unlike the ones in his mother's home-made sandwiches – full of energy and waiting to 'BOING!'.

Hamish's guided tour of Tall Hall was certainly fast and consisted more of grunts and single words rather than fully formed sentences, all spoken in broad Scots: '. . . another bathroom . . . bedroom . . . bedroom . . . damp patch . . . wardrobe . . .' Although Eddie was probably taller than him, he found it difficult to keep up with the little nose-bopping Scotsman.

'How long have you been staying here?' asked Eddie as they hurried down yet another flight of servants' stairs at the back of the house (far more cramped than the grand, ornately carved wooden staircase which the owners would usually have used).

'Wuz born here,' said Hamish, charging through an open doorway into a large kitchen.

'But I thought this place had been empty for years.'

'Has been,' said Hamish, marching them past a long kitchen table on which lay apple cores, skins, nutshells and the peel of a wide variety of vegetables, from potatoes to turnips and parsnips. 'We only moved back in t'other day.'

Hamish led him past an open door to a small room with a tiny window. It looked to Eddie like a prison cell.

'What's that?' he asked.

'Game larder,' said Hamish.

'A what?'

'Where they used to hang the poor wee dead animals and birds killed in the hunt,' said the Scot, clenching his fist.

Eddie was half-expecting another punch on the nose, but for being a meat-eater this time. 'Are all your branch of the MacMuckle family tree vegetarians?' he asked.

'Each and every one of us,' said Hamish, with obvious pride.

They were now in a wide passageway. 'What's in there?' asked Eddie, nodding in the direction of an impressive door, studded with black nails.

'Cellar,' said Hamish without stopping.

'Can we take a look?' asked Eddie, thinking back to the cellar at Awful End and all the wine bottles his father had opened and drunk, just so that he could carve the corks. Eddie wasn't a great fan of his father's artistic endeavours – the truth be told, he thought his father was a dreadful painter and an appalling sculptor – but he admired his dedication.

'Can't go down there,' said Hamish.

'Why not?' Eddie asked.

'We havenae found the key yet.'

'Oh,' said Eddie, a little disappointed.

The tour continued.

Eddie had to admit, to himself at least, that he was in two minds about the strange predicament he'd found himself in. On the one hand, he thought it was a shame that this extraordinary house, in such beautiful surroundings, might not actually belong to his family, and that some of the wonderful pieces of furniture and bits-and-bobs/knick-knacks might not be theirs to keep. On the other hand, the plan was for the Dickenses to sell the house anyway, which meant that it would be lived in by strangers. And, if these MacMuckles had a genuine claim to Tall Hall, wouldn't it be nice that it stayed in Even Madder Aunt Maud's family for its rightful heirs to enjoy?

In other words, he wasn't sure whether he wanted Angus McFeeeeeeee to have to hand over the deeds of the property and land to Alexander MacMuckle or not. And he had no idea how long such a thing might take to happen in Scottish Law anyway.

He knew that English Law (also with a capital 'L') could be a very slow process. Once a local schoolteacher had tried to sue when Mad Uncle Jack had grown a particularly ugly hybrid vegetable and named it after him. Some gardeners made it their life's work to grow new varieties of flowers and vegetables, with varying degrees of success. Mad Uncle Jack's cross between a pea and some root vegetable or other had come about accidentally and the result looked like a very large, very hard and very knobbly pea; the kind of evil giant pea that would be discovered pulling levers behind a curtain at the end of a film in which vegetables were rising up against their human masters.

Mad Uncle Jack had decided to give a name to this extraordinary new vegetable, which didn't taste too bad if boiled long enough and was served with plenty of salt, ground black pepper and butter. Eventually, he settled on 'Lance Peevance' because, as he later explained in the local court, 'Peevance incorporates the pea element of my triumphant vegetable-child, and it is also the name of that man there,' he paused to point at the schoolteacher who was also in court that day because he'd brought the legal action against Eddie's great-uncle, 'who bears more than a passing resemblance to it.'

Lance Peevance – the man not the vegetable – had, by now, had quite enough of Mad Mr Dickens and tried to make a lunge at him, screaming: 'I'll get you yet, Dickens!' which didn't please the judge.

The judge was already on Mad Uncle Jack's side, as it happened. Although schoolteachers were well-respected members of society and seen as 'better' than scullery maids, for example, they still had to *work* for a living. Mad Uncle Jack, on the other hand, was a true gentleman *and* lived up at the big house, which meant that, in the judge's eyes, he should really be allowed to do what he liked and that included calling ugly vegetables after Mr Peevance.

Having said that, both Mad Uncle Jack's and Mr Peevance's lawyers wanted to make as much money from the case as possible, so kept on raising very complicated legal objections on both sides, and sending each other very expensive letters (which their respective clients would, of course, eventually have to pay for).

After three and a half years, judgement was finally passed in Mad Uncle Jack's favour and Lance Peevance was ruined. As a result, he owed his lawyer and the courts so much money that he fled the country disguised as a bag of coal.

On a matter of principle, Mad Uncle Jack paid for WANTED posters to be printed at his own expense. On them was an artist's impression of his own new variety of vegetable, under which were the words:

HAVE YOU SEEN A MISSING SCHOOLTEACHER, WITH MORE THAN A PASSING RESEMBLANCE TO THIS VEGETABLE?

As a direct result of seeing a copy of the poster, a Briton holidaying in France later recognised Lance Peevance and had him arrested. Mad Uncle Jack felt that this was proof, if proof were needed, that calling his vegetable-child 'Lance Peevance' in the first place had been completely and utterly justified.

Amazingly, a few years back, this very trial was turned into a modern (and somewhat avant-garde) opera called *Vegetation Litigation!* for a TV series on one of those arty satellite channels, but the names of the people were changed to ones that were easier to rhyme with 'vegetable patch' and 'court case'.

Back in Tall Hall, however, Eddie's tour was about to be cut short by the sudden arrival of Angus's son Magnus McFeeeeeeee.

'Victoria!' he shouted, bursting into the great hall which Eddie and Hamish were crossing whilst the others were still deep in conversation around one end of the huge table. 'Queen Victoria!' He'd obviously been running and was dripping with sweat. He had a stitch and was clutching his side. He took in great gulps of air, then spoke again. 'She's paying a visit!'

Episode 7

Something in the Air

*In which Eddie gets to confront a suspect
and consume some rather nice cake*

Two days had passed since Magnus
MacMuckle had burst into Tall Hall with his
extraordinary news. At first, everyone had
assumed that he'd meant that Queen Victoria was
turning up at the hall unannounced at any
moment. Then it became clear that he meant that
Her Majesty was paying a visit *to the area*, and not
then and there, but the following week.

Eddie was excited because he'd never laid eyes
on his monarch and was hoping to catch a glimpse

of her at the very least. Perhaps she'd arrive at the same station he had, but on her special royal train (so she could sit on her special lightweight portable travelling throne), and he could be in the crowd waving a small Union Flag – which he had learnt was the correct name for the Union Jack when it was being flown on land.

Angus McFeeeeeeee seemed excited in the same way, making comments such as 'Can ya imagine it? Our own dear queen comin' to these parts?' But Eddie wasn't so sure about the MacMuckles. They seemed to be experiencing a different kind of excitement.

When Eddie was older and recalling the events that happened that year in Scotland, he wrote: 'Looking back on it, it is obvious that their reaction was very different to ours.' Hindsight – looking back on events with the knowledge you could only have after they'd happened – is a very fine thing, but it's true to say that there was certainly something about the MacMuckles' reaction that made him very uneasy.

Another thing which bothered Eddie was young Magnus McFeeeeeeee's reaction on discovering Tall Hall full of strangers. Unlike his father, who'd been surprised, Magnus didn't even ask who anyone was. It was almost as if he knew them already. And now, two days later, Eddie decided to approach him on that very subject.

Magnus McFeeeeeeee was outside the back door of his home scraping dried mud off a pair of his father's walking boots with an old butter knife.

'You already knew that the MacMuckles had moved into Tall Hall, didn't you?' said Eddie, coming up behind him from the garden and leaning over his shoulder. Magnus jerked back in surprise.

'Ya shouldnae creep up on people, English,' he said. 'Did your mammie no teach ya manners?'

'You haven't answered my question,' said Eddie.

'Is that what that was?' said Magnus, busying himself with the boots.

'You weren't surprised to see them there. The truth be told, I was wondering whether the message about the Queen was more for them than for me and your father,' said Eddie.

'I walk into the house to find me da and half a dozen other folk seated at a table. For all I know they're furniture removers or people come to see the house with a view to buy. There's no mystery.'

'If this were a town, I might believe you,' said Eddie, above the noise of scraping knife on mud and boot, 'but in the countryside everyone knows everyone's business – unless they deliberately want it kept secret. You'd have known if there were furniture movers or prospective buyers around! And then there's the matter of how the MacMuckles got into the hall in the first place.'

Magnus avoided his gaze.

'Aha!' said Eddie triumphantly. 'So I was right! You lent them the key, didn't you? As my family's lawyer, your father holds the key to Tall Hall and you must somehow have "borrowed" it and given it to the MacMuckles.'

'Then how did my father come to have the key in order for ya to open the door yusself, the other day, English? Answer me that.'

Eddie had already thought of that before he'd confronted Magnus, so had an immediate response. 'The MacMuckles must have made a copy. All they had to do was press the original in some melted wax or a cake of soap to make a mould.'

The lawyer's son was clearly impressed. 'You've thought of everything,' he said.

'Do you deny it?' asked Eddie.

'I neither deny nor admit anything, English,' said Magnus. The blade of the butter knife flashed in the weak sunlight. He sounded like a lawyer.

'Didn't you stop to think what this might do to your father?' asked Eddie. 'What if these people had stolen everything from the hall or wrecked the place? Your father would have been held responsible. He's supposed to be looking after it.'

'He's no father of mine,' muttered the boy.

'Magnus?' called Mrs McFeeeeeeee's voice from the parlour. 'Have you not finished your father's boots yet?'

'Nearly, Mother,' Magnus called back. 'But English keeps gettin' in me way.'

'Who?' called his mother.

'Edmund,' replied Magnus, sheepishly, just as Mrs McFeeeeeeee appeared at the back door. 'I said Edmund.'

Magnus's mum was holding her large ladle again. 'Sure you did, son,' she said. 'Now you've got the mud off, perhaps you'd be kind enough to give them a good polish?'

'I'll be sure to, Mother,' said Magnus, deliberately stepping on Eddie's toe as he stomped off around the side of the house.

'Come and sit with me, Master Edmund,' said Mrs McFeeeeeeee. 'We'll have some cake and talk about the Queen's visit. It'll be one of the most exciting things ever to have happened around here.'

The cake was excellent. There was no denying that Eddie enjoyed some of the best food he'd ever eaten whilst staying with the McFeeeeeeees. The conversation was most interesting too. It turned out that Mrs McFeeeeeeee knew someone who knew someone who knew someone who knew Sir James Clark. Now, that's not very interesting unless you know that Sir James – another Scotsman – either was or used to be the Queen's Personal Physician (which is a posh title for the Queen's Own Doctor).

'I'm sure he'd fit in well at Awful End,' said Mrs McFeeeeeeee, who had – as you may have gathered from her earlier comments – had the pleasure (?!) of meeting Mad Uncle Jack and Even Madder Aunt Maud on their one joint trip to Tall Hall, and had no illusions about their sanity. 'Apparently he's quite mad. I have it on good authority that he's little more than a naval doctor but, as a friend of Her Majesty's mother, somehow landed himself this plum job!' She offered Eddie another piece of cake. He couldn't resist.

'Thank you,' said Eddie. A cake without broad beans or springs was a rare treat.

'I also have it on good authority that Sir James is a great believer in fresh air as the cure for all ills but is highly suspicious of foliage. I'm told that he planned to have Buckingham Palace pumped full of air to protect it from the surrounding trees which were, he was convinced, clogging up the atmosphere!'

'Did Her Majesty agree to it?' asked Eddie, his mouth full. Although Eddie's mother, Mrs Dickens, was well known for speaking with her mouth full – whether it was with ice-cubes, onions, acorns or even dressing-gown cord tassels – it was not encouraged in the Dickens household, and shows just how delicious Mrs McFeeeeeeee's cake was and just how interested Eddie was in the topic of conversation. Royal gossip was as popular back then as it is now.

'I believe that Her Majesty was on the verge of agreeing to the plan when Sir James brought in another physician, a Dr Arnott, to give additional advice. All was going fine until Dr Arnott confided to the Queen his strong belief that the average person could live for hundreds of years if only he had the maximum amount of fresh air!'

Just in case you're under the impression that Mrs McFeeeeeeee's friend-of-a-friend-of-a-friend (or whoever) was pulling her leg, let me assure you that everything she said was pretty much true. Both Dr Arnott and Sir James Clark were fresh-air freaks. Sir James was also, by all accounts, a pretty rotten doctor. On one occasion he diagnosed Queen Victoria as having a bad attack of indigestion, but it turned out to be typhoid. On another – much more serious – occasion he pronounced one of the Queen Mother's ladies-in-waiting was pregnant when her tummy swelled up. She was unmarried and this caused a terrible scandal and she lost her job, despite her claims that she *couldn't* be pregnant. It later turned out that the poor young woman (whose name was Lady Flora Hastings) wasn't pregnant at all but had cancer of the liver, which was eventually correctly diagnosed by someone else. The good thing was that she had cleared her name. The sad thing was that the cancer killed her soon after.

Mrs McFeeeeeeee talked on, and Eddie listened with rapt attention. Meanwhile, not five miles away, in an abandoned crofter's cottage – yup, you're right, it was the cottage and not the crofter that was abandoned (the crofter having won a lot of sheep in a card game in the local pub had moved to a better cottage nearer the pub) – a very secret meeting was taking place. The three men present all stayed in the shadows and spoke in hushed tones.

'Do ya have the weapon?' asked one.

'I thought *you* had it,' said the second.

'Do nae worry, I have it,' said the third.

'Are you both clear on your duties?' said the first.

'Aye,' said the second.

'Aye,' nodded the third.

'If anything should go wrong with the first shot . . .' said the first.

'It won't,' said the second.

'There'll be no Scottish blood on our hands,' said the third.

There was a noise from outside. The three men froze, then the first tiptoed over to the window. He lifted the edge of a piece of hessian sacking that had been nailed up in front of the window to create a curtain. He looked through the grimy glass into the failing light of evening. A shaggy mountain goat trotted daintily through what had once been the crofter's small garden, sending a pebble skittering across ground.

'False alarm,' said the first.

'When Victoria comes calling we'll give her a day to remember, all right!' said the second.

'That we will,' grinned the third.

'Careful you don't get the rifle tangled up in your beard, Hamish!' said the second.

'Ssssh!' said the first. 'No names, remember.'

Hamish grinned again. The rifle he was holding was taller than he was.

Episode 8

A Highland Fling

*In which plans are made and
we meet the Q-PUS*

In the days that followed, more news about
Queen Victoria's forthcoming visit became
known. She'd be staying on the Gloaming estate
(just a mile or so to the west of Tall Hall) at
Gloaming Castle as a guest of Sir Rumpus Rhome
(pronounced 'Room'), who was an absentee
landlord. This meant that although he owned
hundreds of acres of the surrounding countryside,
he actually lived somewhere else completely. In Sir
Rumpus's case, this was London, where he also

owned large tracts of land. His main residence was Number One Rhome Square, which was always written as Number One with letters, and never with the simple numeral '1'. It was a very beautiful townhouse built in the classical style with stucco pilasters all along the front. (Stucco is plaster meant to look like stone, and pilasters are sort-of fake columns that are for decoration rather than to hold things up.)

Sir Rumpus hated everything about his Scottish estate except for the hunting. He hated the mountains. He hated all that fresh air. And, most of all, he hated the Scots, who 'spoke funny' and, in his opinion, looked at him in a funny way too.

In his opinion – and the only opinion that seemed to matter to Sir Rumpus was his *own* – the Scots were a disrespectful bunch. Sir Rumpus, whom you've probably guessed by now was English, was big on respect. He liked people bowing and scraping before him – and even touching their forelocks if they could find them – and he got plenty of that from people in and around Number One Rhome (pronounced 'Room') Square . . . but these Scottish people seemed much fiercer and more independent. They didn't seem to understand that he was not only English but also a knight – a 'Sir' – which made him doubly superior to them. In fact, he had the worrying suspicion that they did as he instructed only because he was paying them, and they *still* begrudged his presence, which was a sorry state of affairs.

Gloaming Castle still stands today but it's no longer a private house. It's an exclusive Scottish country-house hotel (according to the glossy brochure) and I stayed there for one night when researching the events that you're now reading. I'd like to have stayed longer but the price of half a grapefruit on the breakfast menu was more than I'd normally pay for an entire meal for the two of us, including all the lemonade you can drink.

Number One Rhome Square is no more. Neither is Rhome Square itself, come to that. In the First World War (*a.k.a.* World War One, The Great War or The War To End All Wars) the house was blown up by a primitive bomb dropped from a Zeppelin (which was a big airship). During the Second World War (*a.k.a.* World War Two, or The War That Followed The War To End All Wars), the square was destroyed by a number of bombs dropped from aeroplanes.

After the war, the square was 'redeveloped' and in its place stands a very fine multistorey car park, one of the largest in the city and much appreciated by businessmen and women who would otherwise find it difficult to find parking spaces in the area. It's called 'Rhome Square Car Park' which is the only reminder of what once stood there. Everyone pronounces it 'Rome Square' rather than 'Room Square' which would really annoy Sir Rumpus if he hadn't died a long time ago.

Sir Rumpus Rhome's love of hunting can't be overstated. He loved killing living things and the bigger the better. If he could have found a way of shipping elephants to his Scottish estate just so that he could shoot them he would have. An elephant with antlers would have been the icing on the cake. Some hunters love the thrill of the chase. Sir Rumpus's dictum, however, was: 'The easier the better'. Sometimes he instructed his game-keeper to hide behind a bush with, say, a deer, and to release it just as Sir Rumpus was ready to shoot something. This resulted in more than one gamekeeper being shot in error, which meant even more excitement for Sir Rumpus and a small bonus for the injured men.

Queen Victoria and her party – which meant the people who travelled with her, and didn't necessarily involve balloons and loud music – would be spending a weekend at Gloaming and her visit would include watching an afternoon's hunting.

Of course, Her Royal Highness Queen Victoria would not actually be taking part in the hunt. Oh, no. She had very clear views on women and hunting. Once, when she learnt that one of her granddaughters had been hunting, she sent her a letter saying, 'I was rather shocked to hear of you shooting,' and 'to look on is harmless, but it is not ladylike to kill animals'. Then she used a brilliant phrase: 'It might do you great harm if that were known, as *only fast ladies do such things*.'

Wow! Obviously, getting the reputation as a 'fast lady' was Not A Good Thing. Sir Rumpus and all the male guests would do the hunting. Victoria and the ladies would simply do the looking on. Sir Rumpus was honoured and delighted.

So were Mr and Mrs McFeeeeeeee. They'd received an invitation. The Q-PUS (the Queen's Private Under Secretary) had been sent up a few days in advance and, in addition to all the bigwigs/big cheeses/top dogs/A-list people who always got invited to such events, had been asked to additionally invite 'colourful local characters'.

Queen Victoria was big on colourful local characters. Her security detail – in other words those in charge of her safety – were not. 'Colourful local characters' often turned out to be 'eccentrics' and 'eccentrics' often turned out to be nutters.

Mr McFeeeeeeee was a pretty safe bet. He not only had a suitably funny Scottish name with an interesting story behind it for Her Majesty to find entertaining – ancestors jumping out of trees and strangling people with their bare hands – but he was also a lawyer and could be relied on to behave and not drop his trousers halfway through the proceeding in order to show the Queen a birthmark on his left buttock, as a previous 'colourful local character'/eccentric/nutter had done at a house party in Yorkshire. (There is a strong possibility that the latter was Mad Uncle Jack's brother George, of burning-down-the-Houses-of-Parliament fame, though his diary entry for that day is barely legible, the ink having been smudged by what appears to be liquid paraffin.)

Mrs McFeeeeeeee would be invited to attend the royal festivities simply because she was Mr McFeeeeeeee's wife. Little Magnus McFeeeeeeee was not to be invited. 'I wouldnae come if I was asked,' he'd told Eddie, spitting on the ground, and Eddie hadn't doubted him for a second.

The Q-PUS had also made inquiries (which are like enquiries but spelt with an 'i') about the owner of Tall Hall. 'The MacMuckle family were known to the late King, and Her Majesty is most eager that the present owner, or his representative, attend,' he told Angus McFeeeeeeee who, as well as being an invitee, had been given the job of suggesting other suitable candidates for invitation to the Q-PUS, and for rounding them up.

'I have the great-nephew of the last surviving MacMuckle staying with me as we speak,' he'd proudly told the Queen's man, 'but he's just a child.'

'Excellent!' said the Q-PUS. 'Her Majesty loves children.' This was fortunate because, by the end of her life, she was to have over forty – yes, *forty* – grandchildren. Imagine if, as a granny, she'd been asked to baby-sit them all on the same night!

'Master Edmund Dickens, for that is the laddie's name, is the self-same wee Edmund who found the stolen Dog's Bone Diamond belonging to the fabulously rich American dog-food tycoon Eli Bowser,' said Angus McFeeeeeeee, rather proudly.

'I'm sure Her Majesty will be most interested to meet him,' said the Q-PUS. 'I seem to remember that a stuffed ferret was somehow involved in the process.' He vaguely recalled having had the newspaper reports of the whole extraordinary affair read to him by the Queen's Private Under Under Secretary (the Q-PUUS) or the Queen's Private Assistant Under Secretary (the Q-PAUS). They looked very similar to each other, so he couldn't remember for sure which it had been.

'Stoat,' said Angus McFeeeeeeee.

'I beg your pardon?' said the Q-PUS.

'It was a stuffed stoat,' explained McFeeeeeeee. 'Not a stuffed ferret.'

'I see.' The Q-PUS nodded, as though this were an important detail. Perhaps it was.

And so plans were made in this way, and the date of the arrival of HRH (Her Royal Highness) drew closer and closer.

A Right Royal Arrival

*In which a jam-filled biscuit and a lone piper
get trodden on by royal feet*

When the day of the Queen's visit finally arrived, the headteacher – well, the truth be told, the *only* teacher – of the local school had not only written a special song for the occasion but had also found time it to teach her pupils to sing when HRH Queen Victoria stepped from the royal train on to the green carpet. Yes, of course, it should have been a *red* carpet but, at the dead of night, a group of unidentified anti-royalists had stolen the red carpet, which had been locked in the Station Master's office. By the time Mr McTafferty had discovered the theft, there was no time for him to order a replacement but, making one of those snap decisions that had seen him rise through the ranks of railway company employees, he decided that a green carpet was better than no carpet at all, and had 'borrowed' the stair carpet from Mrs MacHine's cottage who, being in hospital with injuries sustained from being flattened by a woodworm-ridden grand piano, wouldn't notice it had gone. Or so he hoped.

With the aid of a tailor's tape-measure and a complicated diagram supplied in advance by the Q-PUS, McTafferty had calculated exactly where the door of the Queen's carriage would come to rest and, therefore, where the carpet should be placed. He had just had enough time to run across with the carpet from Mrs MacHine's cottage and unroll it across the platform in position when a cry from one of the crowd indicated that the royal train was coming into view.

Imagine the scene. Go on, *please* imagine the scene. It saves me having to describe it. Think of people in their (Scottish) Sunday best. Think of bunting and Union Flags strung up everywhere, like paperchains come Christmastime. Think of children with freshly scrubbed faces and hair dampened and flattened. Think of a small – a *very* small – brass band with kilted bandsmen, their gleaming instruments glinting in the sun. Can you do that for me? I'm most grateful. Now throw in a buzz of anticipation and a feeling of great excitement and then we can all move on.

The train came to halt with a loud hissssssssssssssssssssssssssss (much louder than the hiss of escaping gas in Episode 1 of *Dreadful Acts*) and the band struck up a suitably stirring tune for the occasion. It reached a crashing climax as the door to the carriage was opened from the outside by two strapping guardsmen in 'traditional' garb, and a royal leg appeared. Then Miss MacTash (the headteacher) raised her baton, and her three rows of smartly dressed pupils began to sing:

· *'Welcome Royal Highness,*
Our mighty Queen Victoria,
You are Britain's finest
Which is why we all adore ya!'

There were a few raised eyebrows and mutterings in the crowd at this last line; some from people who certainly didn't adore her, and some from those who did, but thought that *'we all adore ya!'* wasn't an appropriate language with which to address Her Royal Highness. In fact, not fifteen months later, Miss MacTash was forced to retire from her post at the school a year earlier than she originally planned. This was partly as a result of this song, and partly to do with a playground incident involving one of the youngest – and certainly lightest – children in the school and a golden eagle (one of a local nesting pair).

HRH Queen Victoria, on the other hand, seemed delighted by the welcoming committee and charmed by the small group of singing schoolchildren. She probably wasn't listening to the lyrics, however, because she was distracted by something she'd stepped on which, on closer inspection by the Sergeant-at-Arms who was accompanying her, turned out to be a jam-filled biscuit.

Mrs MacHine was particularly fond of jam-filled biscuits and left them dotted about the house, some deliberately – should the need for a biscuit suddenly come upon her – and some by mistake, when she'd put them down for a moment and forgotten about them, or they'd slipped from the edge of one of her bone-china plates. The offending biscuit, which had to be peeled from the sole of Victoria's boot, was from the latter category. Mrs MacHine must have dropped it on the stairs and, in his hurry to remove her stair carpet, Station Master McTafferty hadn't noticed that it was still attached.

Once removed from the royal boot (her left), the Sergeant-at-Arms handed the flattened biscuit to the Q-PUS, who was walking two paces behind him, who, in turn, handed it to the Q-PUUS, who was walking two paces behind *him*, who, in turn, handed it to the Q-PAUS, who was still emerging from the carriage and, having missed what had happened, assumed that they'd all been handed biscuits by way of a welcome, so ate this one with a beaming smile on his face. That night, he wrote in his diary that it had tasted 'a little leathery', which was hardly surprising under the circumstances (or under the royal boot).

Now Lord Rhome (pronounced 'Room') stepped forward and bowed deeply. 'Welcome, Your Majesty,' he said, eyeing the green carpet with some puzzlement before straightening up again. 'My coach is at your disposal,' he added, indicating its whereabouts with a dramatic flourish of the arm. It would have been hard for her to have missed it. The green stair carpet ended at a gate at the edge of the platform, opening on to the road where His Lordship's fine black coach stood, the door held open by a liveried footman. (Liveried has nothing to do with describing Eddie's father's paintings, which usually had a liver-sausagy look about them, but means that the footman was in a special footman's uniform.) As the name suggests, footmen either ran after the coach on foot or jumped up on to special running plates at the back of the coach and stood there (on their feet). Only a coachman actually got to sit on the thing and drive it.

Those not familiar with the area would have assumed that the two liveried – there's that word again – footmen were those usually employed by Lord Rhome at his Gloaming estate, but they'd be wrong. These two men were, in fact, what we'd today call 'undercover policemen'; highly trained to protect the monarch from any surprise attacks. They were from New Scotland Yard in London, the old Scotland Yard (which they'd called plain Scotland Yard, after the palace used by visiting Kings and Queens of Scotland back in the days before Scotland was ruled by the English) having been blown up by Fenians in May 1884, which was somewhat embarrassing for the policemen who worked there because their job was to put a stop to that kind of thing. It's a bit like a fire-prevention officer's office burning down. You feel sorry and all that, and are glad that he managed to save the goldfish in time, but it's funny in a way too. Or, at least, the *idea* of it is. If you're wondering what Fenians (pronounced as though spelt F*ee*nians) are, I don't blame you. You've probably guessed that they were people of some sort, which is a good guess, but I should explain that they were Irish people, and not only Irish people, but also Irish people who generally didn't like the idea of the British monarchy and the British Government – the one with the capital 'G' – ruling Ireland, which made Fenians particularly unpopular with the English authorities, who thought that they had every right to be ruling Ireland because – er – England, Scotland and Wales combined to make a bigger island than Ireland . . . so there! (Or something like that. Who knows?)

Oh, whilst we're on the subject of islands, let me quickly point out something strange which occurred to Eddie when he once saw an actor-manager named Mr Pumblesnook performing a piece from one of Shakespeare's plays, a few years previously. In it was a soliloquy about England

103

which included the words '*this sceptered isle*', which was a bit odd because it occurred to Eddie that England wasn't an isle – an island – at all. It had land borders with Scotland and Wales. Spain had land borders with just two countries too, and nobody called *it* an island, so what was going on? He'd asked Mr Pumblesnook about it but the actor-manager had muttered something about 'never questioning the mighty bard' and had hurried away to stop his wife, Mrs Pumblesnook, doing whatever it was she liked to do with the blotches of skin she peeled off her face and kept in a special pocket until the time was right.

As Queen Victoria made the short journey along the green stair carpet, the cheers of the crowd mingled with a few cries of 'Go back to England where you belong!' (followed, in each instance, by a muffled thud of the offending shouter being merrily bopped on the head by a smiling policeman in dress uniform) ringing in her ears, a lone piper stepped out at the side of Lord Rhome's coach and horses. He was very tall, and very impressively dressed, and was jumped on by the two liveried footmen before you could say, 'They're really two policemen in disguise.'

The two men, Mr Digg (with two 'g's) and Mr Delve, threw themselves at the Lone Piper, knocking the wind out of him and his set of bagpipes, which whined a like flatulent cat, and if you don't know what 'flatulent' means, I'm not going to be the one to tell you. The Lone Piper – who really was a lone piper – wrestled with his attackers, assuming that they were assassins in disguise, planning to harm Her Majesty, whilst Digg (with two 'g's) and Delve wrestled with *him,* assuming that *he* was the assassin in disguise.

The reasons for this fracas – nice word, huh? It means 'noisy quarrel' or 'brawl' and comes from the French word *fracasser,* 'to shatter' – were a direct result of a last-minute change of plan and a failure to communicate. As those of you who can remember as far back as the first page of Episode 1 will recall, Queen Victoria loved all things Scottish, and a lone piper (*a.k.a.* a bloke on his own with a set of bagpipes) was just the sort of thing which added so significantly to her Scottish enjoyment. Unfortunately, however, the lone piper the Q-PUS had had lined up – sorry about the two 'had's in a row, but I didn't invent the language – had – blimey, there's another one – caught a rare kind of flu which you could only catch off a certain breed of pig if you spent too much time with one, so was currently tucked up in bed with a cuddly toy rabbit and a temperature of 104. The cuddly toy rabbit was described as being his mascot, and the temperature of 104 as being dangerous. What the Q-PUS had forgotten to tell those protecting Victoria was that he'd managed to find a last-minute replacement. It was this last-minute replacement whom Mr Digg (with two 'g's) and Mr Delve were now sitting on.

I'd like to be able to tell you what the Lone Piper was saying – and, even with his broad Scottish accent, it was clear enough for the Scotland Yard men to include in their report – but I can't repeat it here because it was t-o-o r-u-d-e. The Lone Piper was very, very, *very* angry. Eddie had witnessed the whole thing from his vantage point at the roadside, where he stood with Mrs McFeeeeeeee on one side and Mr McFeeeeeeee on the other. All three of them were dressed in their almost best, so that they could change into their very best for the main reception.

When Queen Victoria came through the open gate on to the road, she was either so busy acknowledging the crowd with a gentle nod or the very slightest wave of a royal hand or so well trained as not to let such things faze her that she simply stepped on to the Lone Piper, who was struggling on the ground, and into Lord Rhome's coach, the Sergeant-at-Arms doing the same.

When the coach pulled away, heading for Gloaming Castle, the Q-PUS explained to Digg (you must be familiar with the spelling by now) and Delve that the Lone Piper was indeed not only a genuine lone piper but, when he wasn't piping alone, also a retired captain in the British Army. The poor man had been trampled by so many feet that he woke up with some very interesting bruises the following morning. By way of an apology, he was later sent a boxful of figs. They gave him an upset tummy.

Once at Gloaming Castle, Queen Victoria was offered what, according to the itinerary, was 'light refreshment' but, by today's standards, would be better described as 'a pig-out'. There seemed to be course after course, ending with a see-through jelly filled with flower petals. Only the select few were invited to this stage of the proceedings: members of the Rhome family and those making up the shooting party. In other words, after lunch they'd either go out shooting or go out and watch the shooting. The main reception for all the local dignitaries (and Eddie) was scheduled for the evening.

Eddie couldn't wait for the evening to come so, to take his mind off things, he decided to go to Tall Hall to see how things were. Well, 'to see how things were' was the reason that Eddie would have given if he'd been asked why he was going up there again; having been a number of times since he'd first discovered the so-called MacMuckle clan squatting there. I've no doubt that the real reason smelt of heather and had a pretty smile.

Eddie found the front door locked, and no one answered his repeated knocking. Skirting around to the back of the house and down a short flight of stone steps, he found that the door leading into the kitchens wouldn't budge either. But he knew where they hid the key. He ran back up the steps and over to a flowerbed. Lifting a large piece of stone that, by the look of the carvings on it, must once have been part of an older building, he wrestled the rusty old key from a colony of woodlice (or should that be 'woodlouses'?) and let himself in.

The place seemed deserted and, although Eddie had at least as much right as the others to be there, if not more so, it felt a little as though he were trespassing.

'Hello?' he called, his voice echoing 'o', 'o', 'o' through the vast hall. Nothing. After a quick scout around, Eddie was on the verge of giving up and going when he heard some muffled thuds coming from . . . coming from where, exactly?

Not Quite What It Seems

In which Eddie makes a discovery and the author
writes the longest episode in the book

The noises finally led Eddie Dickens to the large studded door; the one which little Hamish had told him led down to the cellar; the one for which Hamish had told him they'd been unable to find the key.

Someone must have found the key, though, Eddie thought, because noises were most definitely coming from down there.

He banged on the door. 'Hello!' he shouted. The muffled thudding continued on the other side. 'Hello!' he shouted once more, then added: 'Are you all right?'

Then he heard the most extraordinary cry . . . or snort . . . or something. He wasn't even quite sure whether it was human or not.

Eddie grabbed a stool and scrambled up on to it, feeling along the top of the door frame to see whether the key had been put there out of view. No luck.

His heart was pounding faster now. He had a terrible sinking feeling. He'd believed that those claiming to be MacMuckles *were* MacMuckles and had even instructed Angus McFeeeeeeee to let them stay here at Tall Hall against the lawyer's advice . . . but what if they were, in truth, a band of villainous impostors involved in some dreadful scheme, and they were using this very cellar as a dungeon, packed with prisoners?

No. Eddie mustn't let his imagination run away with him. How often did one run into villains in real life? Well, in Eddie Dickens's case, quite frequently. He'd encountered the Cruel-Streaks, who were a very nasty family running an orphanage for their own betterment, rather than the poor orphans'; he'd been kidnapped by escaped convicts up on a misty moor; he'd foiled an attempted jewel robbery aboard ship . . . So, seeing as how he seemed to attract trouble like a picnic attracts ants and wasps, no, it *wasn't* beyond the realms of possibility that he was right about being wrong about these so-called MacMackles.

But what should he do? There was no way that he could get that cellar door open without a key and, until he knew what lay behind it, he wasn't happy about the idea of going around accusing anyone of anything.

What if there were a perfectly good explanation for all that terrible thudding . . . though he was very hard pressed to think of one. Perhaps he should go and find Mr McFeeeeeeee and see what he thought. The grounds of Tall Hall bordered the Gloaming estate. Tall Hall was the nearest building to Gloaming Castle, where, at that very moment, Queen Victoria and her party were residing.

Then Eddie had another even more worrying thought. What if it were the MacMuckles who were locked in their own cellar? What if anti-royalist intruders had somehow overpowered Alexander, Iain, Hamish, Martha, Nelly and Roberta – sweet Robbie – and locked them all in there, binding and gagging them so that they couldn't cry for help?

Eddie had been bound and gagged once. Admittedly that had been in an open rowing boat rather than a cellar, but he imagined that the experience must be pretty similar: unpleasant.

Eddie pressed his ear flat against the thick wooden door. He didn't know what he was listening to, but he didn't like what he heard.

Eddie was within a cat's whisker's width of deciding that, whatever the consequences and however embarrassed he'd be if there were a perfectly innocent explanation for scuffling and thudding in the locked cellar, he must tell *somebody* when he heard voices. Someone was coming.

There were few places to hide in the corridor but one was all he needed. Eddie crouched down behind an enormous Chinese-looking vase, taller than a man, with the pattern of a blue dragon snaking across the front.

No sooner had he ducked out of sight than, peering around the bulbous middle of the china monstrosity, he saw Nelly and Martha coming into view.

'Don't look so worried,' Martha said to Nelly. 'It'll soon be over and the Queen will be gone.'

'If it goes wrong, we could all end up in the Tower!' said Nelly, sounding as worried as she looked; her face puffy and her eyes red.

'The boys have been over the plans a hundred times,' Martha tried to reassure her. 'And the cause is a good one.'

'But the rifle –'

'It's been especially adapted. It won't fail.'

'It can't fail, or we'll end up with Scottish blood on our hands,' said Nelly.

They disappeared into the larder.

Eddie's heart was pounding in his ears like a jack-hammer. No, hang on: the *sound* of Eddie's heart was pounding in his ears like a jack-hammer. If his heart really had been in his ears he'd have been in an even worse state than he was. Which was pretty bad.

'*If it goes wrong, we could all end up in the Tower!*' Nelly had said. The Tower of London. That's where they used to send traitors before their execution, Eddie thought. And what treason did the so-called MacMuckles have planned? What had Martha said? '*It'll soon be over and the Queen will be gone.*' That was it. Gone? Gone where?

Eddie had a very uneasy feeling about this; a

stomach-churning, sicky-sick feeling. The occupants of Tall Hall were obviously mixed up in some very unsavoury scheme.

When Eddie was satisfied that the two MacMuckles (if that was what they really were) were occupied by whatever it was that they were doing in the larder, he decided that he must make a break for it. Slipping out from behind the vase, he tiptoed past the open larder doorway, knowing that, if either of them were to glance his way, he could be spotted at any moment. With an almost audible sigh of relief, he made it out of the door, up the steps and slipped away through the grounds. He must find the royal shooting party on the Gloaming estate and warn them that someone meant the Queen some serious harm!

*

Lord Rhome stomped across the heather with glee. He was taking part in his two favourite pastimes: hunting deer and showing off his wealth and importance to people who really mattered; and few people mattered to him more than Queen Victoria.

There had been a time when the Queen had pretty much disappeared from public life altogether. This started when her beloved husband, Prince Albert, had died, and it lasted for about twenty-five years. TWENTY-FIVE YEARS? Yup, *at least* twenty-five years. Like Mad Uncle Jack and the Dickens family portraits, Victoria carried a picture of Albert with her wherever she went, after his death (though it probably wasn't stuck to the lining of her coat with a nail or old sticking plasters), and she also went a little – how shall I put it? – odd. That's it: *odd*.

For example, although Albert was dead and buried and not sleeping in his bed, let alone using the chamber pot kept under it, she gave strict instructions that the chamber pot be cleaned every day. And who would dare argue with someone who ruled great big chunks of the world?

Then, in 1887, she'd been on the throne for fifty years – except for when she nipped off it for reasons already outlined – and took part in huge celebrations to mark this 'golden jubilee'. She had such a great time that she decided to get out and about more and have some FUN; which she did, pretty much for the rest of her life, which is how she came to be visiting the Gloaming estate and watching 'Roomy' (as she called Lord Rhome) and the gentlemen guests take part in the shoot.

Because it's all rather relevant to what's about to happen (and I should know what's about to happen because I'm the one who's about to write about it), I think I should give over a few pages to telling you about some of the attempts and so-called attempts that had been made on the Queen's life until then.

In 1840, a chap called Oxford (not to be confused with the *place* called Oxford, which is unlikely because one was a person with the first name of Edward and the other was – and still is, I assume – a city in Oxfordshire, full of dreaming spires and tourists) shot at Victoria and Albert in their open carriage as they were making their way up Constitution Hill. He ended up in a lunatic asylum on the basis, no doubt, that anyone trying to kill the lovely monarch must have been mad.

In 1842, a certain John Francis tried to kill the Queen not once, but twice. One day he shot at Victoria and Albert as they were trundling down the Mall – the long, straight road leading to and from Buckingham Palace – but his pistol didn't fire properly. Because V & A were embarrassed at the idea of anyone wanting to shoot at them, they decided not to tell anybody . . . so the security measures weren't tightened and this meant John Francis could take *another* pot shot at them the next day. This was very considerate of the royal couple and he took advantage of their kindness. The pistol worked this time, but Francis missed and he was caught.

Just over a month later, *another* John tried to shoot the Queen or, at the very least, to get her attention. This was a boy called John William Bean and he'd probably have had better luck if his gun had contained more gunpowder and less tobacco. Nobody said that would-be assassins have to be *smart*.

The next attack wasn't until nearly thirty years later, which wasn't surprising, what with Her Majesty staying at home moping for much of the time, rather than going out and about, making herself an easy target. It was 1872, and a young man named Arthur O'Connor pointed a gun at the Queen as she passed by in her carriage. One of Victoria's many sons, also called Arthur, chased after O'Connor but Victoria's ghillie, John Brown, reached him first and wrestled him to the ground.

Brown – Scottish and hairy despite the lack of a Mac or Mc in front of his name, you will recall – not only got all the public credit and praise from the Queen but also £25 a year for life and a nice big gold medal (just the sort of shiny thing Even Madder Aunt Maud would have loved to have got her hands on). Prince Arthur thought this was jolly unfair because he'd been *just* as brave as Brown and all he got was a measly gold pin and a 'what a good boy you are to your mummy' kind of thank-you. O'Connor's gun turned out not to have been loaded anyway.

Then, in 1882, it was Brown's turn to be pipped to the post in the saving stakes. (That's s-t-a-k-e-s, as opposed to s-t-e-a-k-s. 'Saving steaks' would suggest saving red meat, which would make no sense in this context whatsoever, so why bring it up? What do you mean *I* brought it up, not you? Oh, I see. You have a point there. Sorry. Never let it be said that I don't apologise when I'm wrong.)

Where was I? Aha! March 2nd, 1882. Windsor Railway Station, that's where. The Queen's carriage was waiting outside and a Mc – a Roderick McLean, to be precise – shot at it with real bullets in his gun and everything. John Brown saw this as a chance to be a hero again – and maybe even get another medal – but, unfortunately for him, he wasn't the first to reach McLean and tackle him. No, sir. That honour went to a couple of Eton schoolboys who repeatedly hit Mr McLean with their rolled-up umbrellas until the authorities grabbed a hold of him and dragged him away.

So, with all these attempted assassinations in mind, let us return to the springy heather on the Gloaming estate where rather a lot of people – a number of whom weren't big fans of the English in general and the English monarch in particular – were wandering around carrying BIG RIFLES. It wouldn't be spoiling the action to say that not all of them had shooting deer in mind.

The start of the shoot did not go well for Lord Rhome. The deer seemed to be hiding, which wasn't cricket. Of course, the game of cricket has little to do with shooting deer – except that both were enjoyed by the ruling classes – but 'not cricket' is a phrase. It means not playing by the rules. And, as far as Lord Rhome was concerned, the deer should have been darting about in the open where he could shoot at them; not keeping a low profile. Had the deer themselves been familiar with the phrase, perhaps they'd have thought that what wasn't cricket was these nasty men wanting to shoot them!

If steam really could come out of people's ears, like it does in cartoons when people are about to explode with rage, it'd certainly have been coming out of both of Lord Rhome's (in a very impressive fashion). He was very frustrated, but trying to remain the perfect host in front of the most important guest he could ever hope to have on the Gloaming estate.

'*Cooo-Eeee!*' called a voice, and Rhome turned to see two complete strangers stomping purposefully across the heather towards them. Both appeared elderly. One – a man – was ridiculously thin and seemed to have large fern-like leaves sticking out of every pocket. The other – the woman who had '*Cooo-Eeee*'-ed – was clutching what looked like a stuffed ferret or somesuch thing.

'Sorry we're late,' said the man.

'And who, sir, are you?' demanded Rhome.

Mad Uncle Jack (for, yes, it was indeed he and Even Madder Aunt Maud who'd put in a late appearance in this adventure) pushed aside the large leaf protruding from the top pocket of his jacket, which had been partially obscuring his beakiest of beaky noses. 'Didn't recognise me with my camouflage, huh?' he chortled. 'I wanted to blend in with the local scenery.'

'Who the devil are you, sir?' demanded Lord Rhome, which was fair enough considering that the reason he didn't recognise Mad Uncle Jack had less to do with the 'camouflage' and more to do with the fact that, until that moment, the two men had never met in their entire lives.

There was frantic whispering going on between those surrounding Queen Victoria. There had obviously been a serious breach in security if this strange pair had managed to get in stuffed-stoat-throwing distance of Her Majesty.

One of the many famous things about Queen Victoria was that, no matter where she was, she never looked behind her when she sat down. What I mean is, she never had to look behind her to check that there was something to sit *on*. Wherever she was, there was always a servant ready to slip a chair (usually her throne, I'd imagine) beneath the royal behind.

As Even Madder Aunt Maud came striding towards her now, skirt hitched high and shouting, 'Hello there, Queenie!' Victoria sat down with surprise. An even bigger surprise was that she found herself sitting on nothing and then ended up on the ground with quite a thud.

The man who had been holding the chair had abandoned his post in order to keep the frightening woman away from his beloved queen. He was now being prodded with Malcolm's nose for his pains.

Talking of pains, how was Her Majesty? Fine. It wasn't the contact between bottom and ground that had shocked her, or even the loss of dignity. It was the fact that for the first time in her entire reign she'd gone to sit down and there hadn't been a chair. It was like the sky suddenly turning green, or water suddenly flowing uphill. Such things just *didn't* happen.

'Quite extraordinary,' she was muttering as she was helped to her feet. 'Quite remarkable.'

'The last of the MacMuckles!' shouted a running man in livery, appearing from the direction in which Mad Uncle Jack and Even Madder Aunt Maud had just appeared.

A startled look crossed the faces of a number of the gun-carriers who were accompanying the royal party on the shoot; including a small, red-bearded chap who looked very keen to punch anybody and everybody on the nose.

The Sergeant-at-Arms stepped forward to confront the running man whilst Mr Digg and Mr Delve, plus the Q-PUS and various others, created a protective ring of people around the Queen.

'This lady and gentleman are the Dickenses,' the man explained. 'Mrs Dickens is the last of the MacMuckles of Tall Hall by the MacMuckle Falls . . . They are late invitees, and wouldn't wait for me to accompany them up here.'

'Aha!' said Lord Rhome at the mention of Tall Hall. He'd been listening in on the conversation. Now it all made sense. This beaky man was a gentleman and a landowner and that made all the difference. He shook Mad Uncle Jack's hand. 'Welcome,' he said.

'I like your hat,' said Mad Uncle Jack.

'Er, thank you,' responded Lord Rhome, who wasn't actually wearing one.

Even Madder Aunt Maud, meanwhile, was trying to speak to Victoria through the legs of those standing between her and the Queen.

'Ow, come on out, you know you love me!' she said teasingly.

For those of you shocked by her obvious lack of respect and deference towards Her Royal Highness, I should make it clear that Even Madder Aunt Maud had mistaken Victoria for someone else. You may find this hard to believe, particularly when she greeted the Queen with a cheery 'Hullo there, Queenie!' but therein lies a clue. When Even Madder Aunt Maud was still plain Mad Aunt Maud, she'd had a friend named Charlotte Hailstrom who bore a striking resemblance to Victoria and had, as a result, earned the nickname 'Queenie'. Unfortunately, this meant that Queen Victoria bore a striking resemblance to Charlotte Hailstrom and, having never met HRH before and having not seen Charlotte for many years, Even Madder Aunt Maud simply assumed that she was her old friend Queenie.

Of course, Queen Victoria had no way of knowing this and, on top of still recovering from the shock of sitting down on nothing more than thin air, was hoping beyond hope that someone would make the worrying woman go away!

Now, let me freeze the action as only an author can – or a reader too, if you simply stop reading; that's one of the great things about books – and explain how MUJ and EMAM come to be here right at the end of this first Further Adventure.

It's simple really. Had they been at Tall Hall when the Q-PUS had sent out the invitations on Angus McFeeeeeeee's recommendations, they'd automatically have been invited but, in their absence, Eddie had been invited to the evening reception in their place. When McFeeeeeeee had written to Mad Uncle Jack about the bunch of people living in Tall Hall, claiming to be not only MacMuckles but also its rightful owners, Mad Uncle Jack had changed his plans and decided to come up to Scotland after all. McFeeeeeeee had then informed the Q-PUS who, in turn, had arranged an invitation for 'Mad Mr Dickens' to attend the shoot and reception with his wife.

What *had* McFeeeeeeee been thinking? He had no excuse. He'd met them before! He *knew* what they were like . . . and, yet, here they were.

'Stag!' went up a cry, bringing us firmly back into the action.

Suddenly, all thoughts of strange latecomers were forgotten. Now, at long last, Lord Rhome might have the chance to shoot some deer.

The beast – large red and antlered – was some way off and appeared to be staring straight at the shooting party with unblinking eyes. It had emerged from behind a rocky outcrop.

The small, red-bearded Scot, whom Eddie had known as Hamish MacMuckle, stepped forward and handed Lord Rhome a rifle.

'Murder!' cried a voice. 'Kidnap!' and Eddie Dickens came into view, being chased by a swarm of policemen.

The stag disappeared behind the rock again, and Lord Rhome fumed once more. 'Piccadilly Circus!' he groaned. 'This is busier than Piccadilly Circus!'

Thwarted Plots!

*In which Eddie is both wrong and right
and Malcolm plays his part*

It was fortunate for Eddie that his great-aunt and great-uncle were on the scene when he arrived. They were able to confirm his identity and to avoid him being wrestled to the ground, or worse, as a possible would-be assassin.

'Her Majesty's life is in terrible danger!' Eddie shouted, trying to escape the police sheep snapping at his ankles.

He – What do you mean, 'What are police sheep?' Oh, good point. Let me clear this one up as quickly as possible so that we can move on. There's something called distemper which is a type of water-based paint, but ignore that. There's something else called distemper which is, according to *Old Roxbee's Book of Doggy Ailments*, 'a highly contagious viral disease involving a high fever and yucky gunky stuff coming from the nose and eyes'. At least, *canine* distemper is, and that's what all the local police dogs were suffering from at the time, so the police had quickly trained up some of the local sheep.

Before you start muttering, 'I don't believe a word of it!' and go off and play with your own stuffed stoat in the corner of your hollow cow or dried-fish treehouse, I should like to point out that it's quite common for people to keep sheep as pets and that, once treated like a dog, they start behaving very much like them too. Constable Jock McGlock, whose job it had been to train the five police sheep, was delighted with how they'd responded, but trying to catch Eddie Dickens had been the first real test.

'The MacMuckles aren't MacMuckles. They've got somebody locked in the cellar and they're planning to shoot the Queen with some special rifle,' shouted Eddie, between gasps for air, as he fell to the heathery ground. That had been one long run from Tall Hall to the shooting party.

'Hello, young Edmund,' said Mad Uncle Jack looking down at his great-nephew. 'Is that a recent haircut?'

Fortunately, Mr Digg and Mr Delve stepped in and asked Eddie to explain himself as soon as possible.

As Eddie spoke, he looked around and his eyes widened. There were Mad Uncle Jack and Even Madder Aunt Maud (with Malcolm), Queen Victoria and her entourage, and various well-to-do men there for the shooting and their well-to-do wives standing around watching . . . and then there were those obviously there to assist, with guns, ammunition, refreshing drinkies and the like. What made them stand out from the others were that they were in Scottish dress and very hairy and . . . and one of them was so-called Hamish.

'Arrest that man!' shouted Eddie. 'He's one of the gang.'

Little Hamish put up a good fight. He managed to bop several people on the nose, including himself, and even managed to bite one of the sheep's legs but, much to the pride of Jock McGlock, the sheep gave as good as it got and bit him back. (The truth be told, Eddie was secretly quite proud of *both* of them; what with neither of them being an actual meat-eater!)

'Wait!' bellowed a voice in the distance, and the

stag reappeared from behind the rocky outcrop. It started ambling down the hillside towards them.

As it got nearer it became obvious that this was no 'monarch of the glen' but more of a deer-coloured pantomime horse with a pair of antlers added.

It stopped and the front part lifted off its head. Inside was the man Eddie knew as Alexander MacMuckle, Clan Chief. Despite his comic bottom half, he still made an imposing figure.

Now the back half of the stag separated from the front and stood up. This was Iain-with-two-'i's-unlike-that-Englishman-Lord-Nelson 'MacMuckle'.

Anyone holding a rifle was now pointing it at the pair of them.

'Will somebody please tell me what's going on?' groaned Lord Rhome, for whom one thing was certain beyond a shadow of a doubt: Queen Victoria would never accept an invitation from him ever again.

'We'll not leave brave wee Hamish to face you on his own,' boomed Alexander. And then explain he did.

The MacMuckles at Tall Hall were not MacMuckles at all. That was true enough, but they weren't out to harm the Queen or anyone else for that matter. Quite the opposite, in fact. Their mission was to prevent harm . . . to the animals.

As a dedicated group of vegetarian animal-lovers, they had pretended to be MacMuckles and rightful heirs to Tall Hall so that they could set up there as part of a plan to save the animals from being shot for sport on the neighbouring Gloaming estate. (At this stage of the telling, Alexander glared at Lord Rhome.) As the English lord wasn't a regular visitor to his Scottish home, they thought they'd have time to develop their plans, until news of the Queen's visit and the shooting party changed everything. They'd already enlisted the help of young Magnus McFeeeeeeee, who was eager to be a party to anything which might upset an English lord, and now he had the added bonus of 'getting one over the English Queen'.

Over the previous few nights they'd been rounding up the deer and wild goats and any other creatures on the Gloaming estate that they feared Lord Rhome and the shooting party might try to kill and had led them all down into the huge cellar under Tall Hall. Although Alexander, Iain, Hamish, Martha, Nelly and Roberta really were vegetarians, much of the fruit and vegetables Eddie had seen being prepared in the kitchens had been to feed the animals.

Once the animals were safe, they'd wanted to find a way to deflect suspicion so that their scheme wouldn't be rumbled even before it had got off the ground. Then they'd found the body of a fine stag in a rocky crevice, which must have somehow lost its footing and fallen to its death. This was when Alexander'd had his brilliant idea: he and Iain would run around dressed as a stag and Lord Rhome would then shoot 'it'. By the time the shooting party reached the spot, though, all they'd find was the body of the already-dead stag.

'You were willing to be shot yourself in place of an animal?' said Mr Digg.

'I don't believe a word of it,' said Mr Delve.

'Then look at Lord Rhome's weapon, man,' said Alexander, indignantly.

This was the hunting rifle little, hairy Hamish had been holding. They soon discovered that it had been adapted to fire nothing more than blanks. So the whole plan had depended on Lord

Rhome shooting the pantomime stag with his doctored weapon. If anyone else had fired real ammunition . . .

Eddie thought back to the conversation between Martha and Nelly and their fears that Scottish blood might be spilled. No wonder they'd been worried. This had been a risky plan!

Alexander and the others had obviously been relying on the fact that the only person who could pull rank on His Lordship was the Queen and, as I pointed out before, she never shot at living things herself.

Whilst everyone else had been gripped in fascination as Alexander explained their failed scheme, still dressed as the front end of a stag with the head tucked underneath his arm, Even Madder Aunt Maud had been showing Malcolm the heather. Now she came upon the huge bearded man quite by chance.

'Oh, hello, Alexander,' she said absent-mindedly. 'How's your sister Martha?'

Alexander grunted some form of acknowledgement through his mighty Scottish beard.

'You know these people?' gasped Eddie.

'Of course. He's Alexander McMickle and there's Iain with three feet.'

'Two 'i's,' Iain McMickle corrected her. 'Good afternoon, Mad Miss Maud MacMuckle.'

'Who are they?' demanded Mr Digg and Mr Delve.

'The McMickles? Loyal servants to the MacMuckles for generations,' said Even Madder Aunt Maud, moving on, 'until my father had some argument with them over a missing egg-spoon and had them all banished from the district.' She was now showing Malcolm a passing bumble-bee.

'Take them away!' sighed Mr Delve, and the policemen (and sheep) that had swarmed up the hillside after Eddie now went down the hillside with Alexander, Iain and Hamish McMickle in custody.

'What will you charge them with?' Eddie asked Mr Digg, as they watched them go.

'Stealing my animals, trespass and imperson-ating a stag, if I have anything to do with it!' fumed Lord Rhome.

'I feel so stupid,' said Eddie. 'I thought they were going to try to harm Her Royal Highness.'

'Better safe than sorry, ay?' said Mr Delve.

But, underneath it all, Eddie couldn't help admiring the McMickles for what they'd tried to do.

★

Nobody could deny that Eddie had been wrong about the so-called MacMuckles, or the McMickles, as they'd turned out to be called – and I should probably point out that 'Many a McMickle does not a MacMuckle make', just to get it out of my system – but I don't want you to go away with the misconception that there wasn't a foiled attempt on Queen Victoria's life that day. There was.

Once the men-dressed-as-deer scam had been revealed, and explained to everyone's satisfaction, no one was quite sure what to do. Lord Rhome was all for having the animals let out of the cellar and shot anyway, but the Queen was appalled at the idea and said so in no uncertain terms. He had been about to suggest that they let loose the police sheep and shoot at them, but decided against it.

'We could dig for truffles,' Even Madder Aunt Maud suggested, thrusting Malcolm into Eddie's arms and throwing herself to the ground, digging in a patch of earth between the clumps of heather. It reminded Eddie of her once digging for a shiny thing in a snowdrift.

Embarrassed as only a child can be by the behaviour of his or her relative, Eddie stood in front of her in the hope that he was blocking her from Queen Victoria's view.

Mad Uncle Jack, meanwhile, was deep in conversation with a man with an impressively twirly moustache. It was a very one-sided conversation, with the man doing little more than grunting and nodding.

This didn't stop MUJ, though, who was thoroughly enjoying himself. He was probably secretly rather pleased that he didn't have to do any actual shooting, being such a dreadful shot. Unfortunately (or not, as we shall see), Mad Uncle Jack suddenly became distracted by a particular clump of heather, the shape of which reminded him of his father's – Dr Malcontent Dickens's – head, at exactly the same time that he was drawing from his jacket pocket the dried swordfish he used as a back-scratcher. Twisting around rather suddenly whilst clutching the fish, he knocked the startled man with the moustache to the ground.

When members of Her Majesty's security detail – yup, Mr Digg and Mr Delve again –

rushed forward to help him up, they noticed that the man's moustache had fallen off, and, being highly trained police officers, they registered that it was unusual for such facial hair to come off in one piece like that, so they were immediately very suspicious. When the man himself noticed his moustache lying on the ground like a very hairy, very dead caterpillar, he tried to make a run for it but the hands which had been helping him to his feet now grabbed him. Mr Digg held his right arm and Mr Delve his left.

It was during this struggle that a pistol fell from one of the man's pockets.

Polite as always, and a little guilty at having accidentally knocked the poor chap to the ground, Mad Uncle Jack bent down and picked the pistol out of the springy heather, with the intention of returning it to the would-be assassin.

'You dropped this, sir,' he announced.

As I've already pointed out more than once, Mad Uncle Jack was not very good with guns and his waving this one around made everyone very nervous.

Particularly Eddie.

'WEAPON!' shouted the Q-PUS when he saw the pistol, causing Mad Uncle Jack to turn towards him to see what all the fuss was about.

As his great-uncle began to turn, Eddie feared the worst and, literally, sprang into action.

'I prefer a pocket knife myself,' Mad Uncle Jack was saying, just as he accidentally pulled the trigger.

In the meantime, Eddie was throwing himself bodily between the Queen and the bullet, which was a very brave, or very foolish, thing to do.

He didn't make it in time.

Fortunately for HRH Queen Victoria and her adoring (English) subjects, Malcolm did.

Eddie had still been holding Malcolm whilst Even Madder Aunt Maud was digging for truffles in the undergrowth. The stuffed stoat had reached Her Majesty before Eddie had, as this freeze-frame diagram below clearly illustrates.

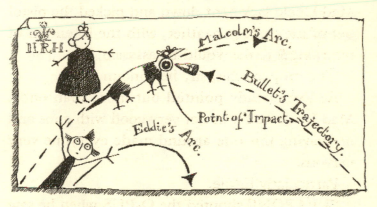

And that is why, six months later, the Dickens family came to be at Buckingham Palace and how

Malcolm the stuffed stoat came to be presented with a medal for bravery by a grateful monarch. Eddie, of course, got nothing. Think back to that incident with John Brown and Prince Arthur. You don't get medals for coming second – well, you do at the Olympics but not when it comes to saving monarchs from potential assassins – and it was Malcolm who took the bullet for her. He didn't seem to mind; Malcolm, that is. Even Madder Aunt Maud had the bullet removed and kept it in a jar on a shelf inside Marjorie. Malcolm, meanwhile, was stitched up and was as good as . . . well . . . certainly not as good as new, but as good as he had been prior to saving the life of the monarch. He didn't get £25 a year for life but, being stuffed, he didn't mind and, being mad, neither did Even Madder Aunt Maud. (She was impressed that her friend Charlotte 'Queenie' Hailstrom lived in such a nice big house, though.)

And what became of the McMickles? The Dickenses where very happy to let them stay in Tall Hall. The McMickle clan had been loyal servants to the MacMuckle clan in the past – I'm not clear what the egg-spoon incident had been which had caused the rift between the two families but it clearly didn't bother Even Madder Aunt Maud – and Mad Uncle Jack and Even Madder Aunt Maud were perfectly willing to give them a (very high) roof over their heads. Eddie was very satisfied that Robbie and her family ended up living there. One of the McMickles' first jobs now that they were legitimately living in Tall Hall was to fence off the grounds so that, once they were released from the cellar, the animals didn't end up straight back on the Gloaming estate where Lord Rhome could take pot shots at them.

Of course, Lord Rhome was furious. After all, they were *his* animals and he had every right to have them back, but the McMickles had a very good lawyer indeed, in the form of Angus McFeeeeeeee, who knew the Scottish Law (with a capital 'S' and a capital 'L') inside out and who kept Lord Rhome's Scottish lawyer (McFeeeeeeee's good friend Marcus MacGoon) busy with endless legal paperwork.

Whenever, on one of his less and less frequent trips to his Scottish estate, Lord Rhome summoned Mr MacGoon, the lawyer kept on reminding him that 'Possession is nine-tenths of the law,' which always threw His Lordship into a terrible rage.

Fighting an English absentee landlord made Angus McFeeeeeeee a hero in his son Magnus's eyes and when, many, many years after this adventure ended, Angus McFeeeeeeee died an old, old man, Magnus McFeeeeeeee gave a very stirring speech in memory of his much-loved dad. Magnus too became a lawyer and campaigned for Scottish independence throughout his life. Today, a McFeeeeeeee sits in the Scottish Parliament. He may be very small but he has a loud voice and strong opinions and makes sure that McFeeeeeeee is spelt with eight 'e's on the order papers.

And that nugget of information almost brings us to the close of this, the first of Eddie's *Further Adventures*.

Almost.

But not quite.

There's the small matter of the MacMuckle Falls or Gudger's Dump. Take your pick. You may recall that this feeble apology of a waterfall was somewhat black and slimy. Small wonder. One morning, about two years after Eddie's eventful visit, it erupted in a fountain of thick, black liquid. The earth had revealed its secret: beneath the grounds of Tall Hall lay one of the very few, if not the *only*, oil deposits on mainland Scotland.

When the McMickles reported this to Mad Uncle Jack, he ordered it plugged. (He even drew a sketch of what he'd like the plug to look like; with a long chain like the one in his favourite bathroom at Awful End.) What did he want with all that oil or the money it could generate? It would only mean that a rig would have to be built, along with roads and buildings and all sorts of other things that would mess up the peaceful life of the Highlands and upset the animals. He was quite happy to leave things the way they were. It was dried fish he was interested in. Not oil.

If you think he was mad to turn down the opportunity to make money – especially when he'd been planning to sell Tall Hall in the first place in order to make some – I need only remind you what members of his family called him: *Mad Uncle Jack* and – do you know what? – I expect that they loved him all the more for it anyway.

It's adventures that make life really worth living, not money. And Eddie had plenty more of those to come.

THE END

until a further Further Adventure

AUTHOR'S NOTE

Some readers have mentioned that they're not sure which parts (if any) of my books are made up and which parts (if any) are true. I know how they feel.

The Philip Ardagh Club

COLLECT some fantastic **Philip Ardagh** merchandise.

WHAT **YOU** HAVE TO DO:
You'll find tokens to collect in all Philip Ardagh's fiction books published after 08/10/02. There are 2 tokens in each hardback and 1 token in each paperback. Cut them out and send them to us complete with the form (below) and you'll get these great gifts:

2 tokens = a sheet of groovy character stickers
4 tokens = an Ardagh pen
6 tokens = an Ardagh rucksack

Please send your collected tokens and the name & address form to:
Philip Ardagh promotion, Faber and Faber Ltd, 3 Queen Square, London, WC1N 3AU.

1. This offer cannot be used in conjunction with any other offer and is non-transferable. 2. No cash alternative is offered. 3. If under 18 please get permission and help from a parent or guardian to enter. 4. Please allow for at least 28 days' delivery. 5. No responsibility can be taken for items lost in the post. 6. This offer will close on 31/12/04. 7. Offer open to readers in the UK and Ireland ONLY.

Name: ....
Address: ....
....
....
Town: ....
Postcode: ....
Age & Date of Birth: ....
Girl or boy: ....

Philip Ardagh Club
token

Philip Ardagh Club
token